P9-DFO-445

AUNT DIMITY AND THE WIDOW'S CURSE

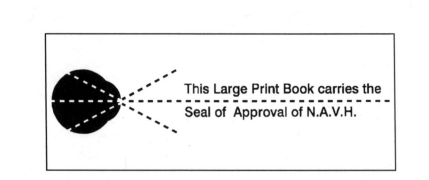

This Large Print Book carries the Seal of Approval of N.A.V.H.

AUNT DIMITY AND THE WIDOW'S CURSE

NANCY ATHERTON

THORNDIKE PRESS

A part of Gale, Cengage Learning

Farmington Hills, Mich • San Francisco • New York • Waterville, Maine
Meriden, Conn • Mason, Ohio • Chicago

GALE
CENGAGE Learning·

Copyright © 2017 by Nancy T. Atherton.
Thorndike Press, a part of Gale, Cengage Learning.

ALL RIGHTS RESERVED
This is a work of fiction. Names, characters, places, and incidents either are the product of the author's imagination or are used fictitiously, and any resemblance to actual persons, living or dead, businesses, companies, events, or locales is entirely coincidental.

Thorndike Press® Large Print Mystery.
The text of this Large Print edition is unabridged.
Other aspects of the book may vary from the original edition.
Set in 16 pt. Plantin.

LIBRARY OF CONGRESS CATALOGING-IN-PUBLICATION DATA

Names: Atherton, Nancy, author.
Title: Aunt Dimity and the widow's curse / by Nancy Atherton.
Description: Large print edition. | Waterville, Maine : Thorndike Press, a part of Gale, Cengage Learning, 2017. | Series: Thorndike Press large print mystery | Series: Aunt Dimity
Identifiers: LCCN 2017016978 | ISBN 9781410495044 (hardcover) | ISBN 1410495043 (hardcover)
Subjects: LCSH: Women detectives—England—Fiction. | Dimity, Aunt (Fictitious character)—Fiction. | Large type books. | BISAC: FICTION / Mystery & Detective / Women Sleuths. | FICTION / Mystery & Detective / General. | GSAFD: Mystery fiction.
Classification: LCC PS3551.T426 A93375 2017b | DDC 813/.54—dc23
LC record available at https://lccn.loc.gov/2017016978

Published in 2017 by arrangement with Viking, an imprint of Penguin Publishing Group, a division of Penguin Random House LLC

Printed in the United States of America
1 2 3 4 5 6 7 21 20 19 18 17

For Emily Wunderlich,
who has the patience of a saint

One

Annabelle Craven was an ideal neighbor. Quiet, tidy, and unfailingly polite, she was the sort of neighbor who could be relied upon to lend a frantic baker a cup of sugar or to water a window box while its owner was away on holiday.

No one knew Mrs. Craven's exact age. She never mentioned it, and it would have been impertinent to inquire, but anyone with eyes could see that she was elderly. Her tweed skirts and blazers hung loosely on her shrunken frame, her soft gray eyes peered out from a face webbed with wrinkles, and she wore her long white hair in a wispy bun on the back of her head. Her tweed skirts and blazers were elderly, too, as were her sensible shoes, but her clothes were well made and well kept and would in all likelihood outlast her.

Mrs. Craven was in remarkably good health for a woman of her advanced years.

Her eyesight was undimmed, her hearing was excellent, and her nimble fingers could undo knots that defeated much younger women. She moved slowly but surely, without the aid of a cane or a walker, and everyone who knew her agreed that her mind was as agile as her fingers. She could hold her own in any conversation and she wasn't the least bit forgetful. If Mrs. Craven made an appointment, she kept it.

Mrs. Craven lived in Finch, a small and somnolent village set among the rolling hills and the patchwork fields of the Cotswolds, a pastoral haven described in countless guidebooks as one of the prettiest regions in England.

I agreed with the guidebooks. My family and I lived near Finch, in a honey-colored cottage on a narrow winding lane lined with tall hedgerows. Although my husband, Bill, and I were Americans, as were our twin sons and our daughter, we'd lived in England long enough to develop a minor addiction to scones, clotted cream, and strawberry jam.

We kept our addiction in check by leading full and busy lives. Bill ran the European branch of his family's venerable Boston law firm from an office overlooking the village green; our ten-year-old sons, Will and Rob, attended Morningside School in the nearby market town of Upper Deeping; and I juggled the challenging roles of wife, mother, friend, neighbor, community volunteer, and chief baby wrangler.

Our daughter, Bess, was thirteen months old and terrifyingly mobile. She kept me on my toes by toddling eagerly toward anything that might kill her. Her death wish list included, but was by no means limited to, stairs, stoves, streams, snakes, wasps, and well-sharpened knives.

The sixth member of our family was Stanley, a sleek black cat with dandelion-yellow eyes. Stanley had a decided preference for Bill, though he was kind enough to tolerate the rest of us. He divided his time between sleeping in Bill's favorite armchair and keeping his long, curling tail out of Bess's reach.

Bill's father, William Willis, Sr., had made our happiness complete when he'd retired from his position as the head of the family firm and moved to England to be near his grandchildren. A genteel and well-heeled widower, Willis, Sr., had broken many a hopeful heart in Finch when he'd married the noted watercolorist Amelia Bowen. The newlyweds lived just outside of Finch, in Fairworth House, a graceful Georgian mansion surrounded by a modest estate.

Mrs. Craven lived in Bluebell Cottage, a tiny gem in the necklace of golden-hued stone buildings that encircled the village green. She'd moved into her small cottage a few years after Bill and I had moved into our somewhat larger one, and I'm ashamed to say that I wasn't on hand to greet her when she arrived. I'd been toilet training the twins at the time — an exercise guaranteed to concentrate the mind — and I'd been too preoccupied with Making Toilet Time Fun to spare a thought for an elderly newcomer.

I'd spared many thoughts for Mrs. Craven since then. I paused to chat with her whenever our paths crossed, and they crossed almost daily. Like the rest of our neighbors, Mrs. Craven and I took tea breaks in Sally Cook's tearoom; joined in the weekly singalongs at Peacock's pub; attended services at St. George's Church; and shopped at Taxman's Emporium, Finch's grandly named general store.

I could also count on seeing Mrs. Craven at the many villagewide events that kept Finch from becoming *too* somnolent. Nothing, not even the changeable English weather, could keep her away from the flower show, the art show, the church fete, and the harvest festival, and she always arrived in plenty of time to snag a front-row seat at the Nativity play. She was famous in Finch for using a pair of antique opera glasses to view the annual sheepdog trials and she seemed to take a great deal of pleasure in watching my horse-mad sons and their friends compete for ribbons in the local gymkhana.

Mrs. Craven had no children of her own and no close relatives. She'd outlived most of her friends and she'd lost her beloved husband to the ravages of Alzheimer's disease. She'd once told me that his lengthy decline and his final passing had prompted her to leave her old village behind and to make a fresh start in a place untainted by painful memories. I'd told her that she'd chosen her new home well.

Everyone in Finch liked Mrs. Craven. Though she didn't own a car, someone could always be found to take her to Upper Deeping to do her banking, to see her doctor, or to hunt for bargains at the Saturday sales. Sally Cook never tired of swapping recipes with her, Dick Peacock named one of his undrinkable homemade cordials after her, and George Wetherhead, the most bashful man in Finch, was relaxed enough in her presence to meet her gaze when they

11

exchanged pleasantries. Mr. Barlow, who served as our local handyman as well as the church sexton, looked after her cottage free of charge, and James Hobson, a retired schoolteacher and an enthusiastic amateur historian, loved to listen to her stories about "the olden days."

Mrs. Craven could have spent every minute of every day in what passed for a social whirl in Finch, but she chose to spend much of her time alone in Bluebell Cottage, pursuing her primary passion: making quilts. She'd turned her sunny upstairs front bedroom into a workroom, but it wasn't the only room she'd dedicated to her craft. She'd lined the dining room, the lumber room, the attic, and the back bedroom with shelves built to her specifications by Mr. Barlow to hold row upon row of clear plastic boxes in which she stored what appeared to be a lifetime's accumulation of vintage fabrics.

Though she kept her best china in a handsome mahogany sideboard in the dining room, she used the equally handsome mahogany table as a work surface. I'd often seen a quilt's three layers — backing, batting, and top — spread one atop the other on the dining room table, awaiting the next phase in production.

The dining room table met Mrs. Craven's requirements because she didn't make full-size quilts. She specialized in baby quilts, and her baby quilts were very special indeed. Each was handmade from start to finish, and no two were exactly alike.

She would have nothing to do with pre-packaged polyester quilt kits or with the insipid appliquéd kittens, puppies, and teddy bears the kits' manufacturers deemed suitable for a nursery. Mrs. Craven used only the softest of cotton fabrics to make brightly colored patchwork quilts in a seemingly limitless array of traditional patterns.

I knew next to nothing about quilt making, but the names of the patterns delighted me. Pastel kittens, puppies, and teddy bears seemed anemic compared with Old Maid's Ramble, Johnny 'Round the Corner, Victorian Fans, Tumbling Blocks, Pinwheels, and Broken Dishes.

Mrs. Craven "signed" her quilts by embroidering each one with a tiny black-and-white cow. She'd once told me that the little cows were a tribute to her father, who'd managed a prize-winning herd of Friesians for a local landowner when she was growing up. My sons made a game of finding the cows in her finished quilts when we visited Bluebell Cottage, and quite a few adults played the same game when she displayed her quilts at the church fete.

Of the many quilts Mrs. Craven created, my favorites were also the rarest. They were what she called her "whole-cloth" quilts. Whole-cloth quilt tops were neither pieced together from scraps nor brightly colored. They were made from a single piece of cream-colored fabric embellished from edge to edge with intricate patterns of meticulous cream-colored embroidery. Celtic knots, entwined hearts, feathers, fans, flowers, leaves, spirals, and shooting stars were but a few of the patterns that found their way into Mrs. Craven's whole-cloth quilts, and while the color palette was undeniably subtle, the needlework was nothing short of extraordinary.

Grant Tavistock and Charles Bellingham, who ran an art appraisal and restoration business from their home in Finch, classified Mrs. Craven as a genius. They could have introduced her to a dozen museum directors who would have jumped at the chance to exhibit her handiwork, but she was too humble even to consider showing her quilts to a knowledgeable curator.

Instead, she sold her small masterpieces from a stall at the annual church fete and donated every pound of the proceeds to St.

George's. Thanks to her fund-raising efforts, the churchyard had a drainage system that could handle heavy downpours, the south porch had a watertight roof, and the lytch-gate had a new set of wrought-iron hinges.

Mothers who were lucky enough to own one or more of Mrs. Craven's quilts tended to keep them well away from their infants, for fear of the stains associated with infants. I'd framed the three whole-cloth quilts I'd purchased from her and hung them on a wall in our master bedroom. To me, they were works of art.

Mrs. Craven couldn't understand what all the fuss was about. She believed that her quilts served a practical purpose and she was a bit disappointed in me for treating them so reverently. She would have been better pleased if I'd allowed my children to chew on them, spit up on them, dribble on them, and anoint them with applesauce, pureed carrots, and other less savory substances. To Mrs. Craven, a well-used quilt was a well-loved quilt.

On a damp Thursday evening in early April, Bess and I spotted our elderly neighbor as she took a seat in one of the folding chairs Mr. Barlow had set up in the old schoolhouse, which had for many years served as Finch's village hall. The flower

15

show, the art show, and the Nativity play were held there, but the orderly rows of folding chairs signaled the advent of a village affairs committee meeting. By the time Mrs. Craven arrived, nearly everyone who lived in Finch was present.

Millicent Scroggins, Opal Taylor, Selena Buxton, and Elspeth Binney — whom Bill had dubbed "the Handmaidens" because of their devotion to his father — sat together in the second row of chairs. I could hear them discussing Sally Cook's new pageboy haircut and whether or not it would suit Christine Peacock. Christine and Sally sat side by side between their respective husbands, making it easy for the Handmaidens to compare neck lengths, brow widths, and cheekbone breadths.

In the back row, Grant Tavistock and Charles Bellingham were deep in conversation with Horace Malvern, a local dairy farmer who wished to commission a portrait painting of his two-year-old grandson, little Horace Malvern III. James and Felicity Hobson had also chosen chairs in the back row, but though they sat together, they were engaged in separate conversations. While Felicity described the layout of her herb garden to Mr. Barlow, James described his newest piece of metal-detecting equipment to Lilian Bunting, who shared his interest in local history.

Lilian was married to the vicar of St. George's Church, but her husband hardly ever attended committee meetings. Theodore Bunting had inadvertently inspired the sin of envy in his flock by receiving a special dispensation from our all-powerful chairwoman, Peggy Taxman, to spend committee evenings at home in the vicarage, where he could enjoy a nice cup of cocoa while he worked out the kinks in the sermon he would deliver on Sunday.

Jasper Taxman and George Wetherhead sat at the long table on the dais that also served as the stage for the Nativity play. Jasper was the committee's treasurer and George was its secretary, but both men were overshadowed by Jasper's formidable wife, Peggy Taxman, who sat regally between them in the chairwoman's chair.

Bree Pym, a young New Zealander who'd inherited a house near Finch from her great-grandaunts, the late and much lamented Ruth and Louise Pym, arrived only minutes before Peggy called the meeting to order. Bree was temporarily on her own because her boyfriend, the noted conservationist Jack MacBride, was on a lecture tour in Scandinavia.

Bree Pym stood out in Finch because of her youth, her spiky hair, her tattooed arms, her pierced nostril, her highly original sense of style, and her refusal to be intimidated by Peggy Taxman. Peggy's gimlet gaze and stentorian harrumphs had absolutely no effect on Bree's behavior. If Bess wanted Bree to chase her around the schoolhouse in a game of Big Bad Bear during committee meetings, Bree would chase her, growling menacingly, regardless of the poisonous looks thrown at her from the dais. Bree was the young aunt I would have chosen for Bess, if I'd had a say in the matter.

Like Bree, Bess and I were temporarily on our own. Easter break was upon us and Bill had decided to put it to good use by taking Will and Rob on a ten-day, boys-only camping trip in the Lake District. To beat the weekend traffic, they'd loaded Bill's car on Wednesday evening and driven off in the wee hours of Thursday morning. I'd waved good-bye to them without the slightest twinge of resentment.

I was perfectly happy to be excluded from their adventure. The Lake District was the rainiest region in England, and while April wasn't one of its rainiest months, I could almost guarantee that April showers would do what they had to do to bring May flowers. The thought of being cooped up in a wet tent with a toddler who was still in diapers didn't fill me with glee.

Even a fair-weather camping trip wouldn't have appealed to me. I could too easily envision Bess toddling merrily into campfires, toasting forks, wasps' nests, and patches of poison ivy to regard camping as anything other than a hospital visit waiting to happen. If Bill and the boys had been spending ten days in a country hotel on the shores of Lake Windermere, I would have been green with envy. Since they weren't, I wasn't.

Mrs. Craven never missed a village affairs committee meeting, and I tried very hard to miss as few as possible. Peggy Taxman, who ran the post office, the general store, the greengrocer's shop, and every committee meeting that had ever been held in Finch, had a nasty habit of "volunteering" absentees for duties that invariably required the use of a broom and a small fleet of rubbish bins. Needless to say, her meetings were always well attended.

Though Mrs. Craven had a spotless attendance record, she contributed nothing to the proceedings. In stark contrast to the rest of the villagers, who could discuss the pros and cons of purchasing a new tea urn for months on end, Mrs. Craven was content to sit in silence while vital decisions were made — usually by Peggy Taxman — about the harvest festival, the church fete, and the other events that filled the village calendar.

I suspected that Mrs. Craven's reticence stemmed from her humility. She was willing to share her opinions with me over a cup of tea in her snug little kitchen, but I couldn't convince her to express them to a wider audience. The limelight possessed no allure for her, and while she seemed to enjoy watching her neighbors engage in lively debates, she was too diffident to add her voice to theirs.

Silence was an alien concept to the voluble villagers, but they respected Mrs. Craven's right to maintain hers. She was such a willing worker that Peggy Taxman didn't feel the need to volunteer her for any task, and no one demanded that she take a stand on a hotly contested issue. In a schoolhouse filled to the rafters with chatter, some of it quite acrimonious, Mrs. Craven was notable only for her reluctance to speak up.

Which was why my jaw dropped — along with everyone else's — when Mrs. Craven got to her feet at the end of the meeting, smiled cordially at Peggy Taxman, and for the first time in living memory, made her voice heard.

Two

"Madam Chairwoman," said Mrs. Craven, "I would like to address the assembly."

A hush fell over the schoolhouse. Every face was alive with polite curiosity. James and Felicity Hobson, who'd been halfway to the door, retraced their steps and sank soundlessly onto their folding chairs. Mr. Barlow unfolded the chair he'd just folded and sat on it. Grant Tavistock resumed his seat somewhat awkwardly, having already threaded one arm through the sleeve of his rain jacket.

Bree Pym, who was crawling after Bess with a menacing growl, ceased growling instantly and sat back on her heels, looking for all the world like a startled meerkat. Unable to arrest her forward momentum, Bess toddled unsteadily into Mr. Barlow's knees. He picked her up, placed her on his lap, and gave her his key ring to play with. The jangling noise sounded unnaturally loud in the suddenly silent schoolhouse.

Peggy Taxman stared at Mrs. Craven wordlessly, which was in itself a rare event. Peggy was seldom at a loss for words, and her comments were usually delivered at a decibel level that could shatter granite.

"Please forgive me, Madam Chairwoman," Mrs. Craven added. "I intended to introduce my proposal under 'other business' but I'm afraid you brought the gavel down before I could speak."

"As usual," said Dick Peacock in a carrying undertone.

"It's quite all right, Mrs. Craven," Peggy boomed, ignoring Dick. If anyone else had attempted to extend a meeting Peggy had adjourned, she would have ignored them as well, but even she had a soft spot for Mrs. Craven. She gave the gavel an authoritative *bang* and bellowed, "The meeting has been reconvened so that Mrs. Craven can tell us about her, er, proposal."

"You're very kind." Mrs. Craven inclined her head respectfully to the chairwoman, then turned to face the room. "My dear friends and neighbors," she began, "a project has been languishing in my attic ever since I moved into Bluebell Cottage. I doubt that I shall live long enough to complete it by myself."

Cries of "Don't be silly!" and "Chin up, old girl!" rang out until Peggy brought her gavel down again.

"What sort of project is it?" Peggy roared.

"It's a quilt," Mrs. Craven replied. "A rather large quilt."

A murmur of comprehension rippled through the schoolhouse. None of us could conceive of Mrs. Craven having anything other than a quilt in her attic.

"I pieced the top together many years ago," Mrs. Craven explained. "I have the backing fabric and the batting material, but I need help to do the actual quilting."

"A quilting bee!" Elspeth Binney exclaimed delightedly. "You're proposing a quilting bee!"

"I am," said Mrs. Craven, smiling. "In the past, quilting bees were a way for rural women to socialize while performing a useful task. While they sewed, they shared joys and sorrows, exchanged news and recipes, and supported one another in times of trouble."

"You're not in trouble, are you, Mrs. Craven?" asked Mr. Barlow.

"If I am, it's the universal trouble of having too much to do and too few hours in the day to do it," Mrs. Craven replied. "I would dearly love to finish my quilt before I run out of time."

"I think it's a lovely idea," said Selena Buxton. "I can't imagine why we haven't done it before."

"I've given some of you private quilting lessons," said Mrs. Craven, nodding to the Handmaidens, "so you can get started straightaway."

"What about the rest of us?" asked Felicity Hobson.

"If you know how to do a running stitch," Mrs. Craven told her, "you won't have any trouble learning how to quilt. And if you don't know how to do a running stitch, I can teach you."

"I can do a running stitch," Christine Peacock allowed, "but my stitches aren't as neat as yours."

"No matter," said Mrs. Craven. "We don't want our quilt to look machine made, do we? Uneven stitches give a quilt character. They prove that it was made by a human being."

"Then you must be a robot, Mrs. Craven," said Charles Bellingham, "because I've never seen an uneven stitch in your quilts."

Mrs. Craven waved away the compliment. "I've had a lot of practice, Charles, but I'm still capable of producing some very crooked lines indeed. If I unpicked every wobbly stitch I sewed, I'd still be working on my first quilt!"

"What a loss that would be," said Grant Tavistock.

The villagers added their praise to his until Peggy silenced them with her gavel.

"You won't have to bring anything but yourselves," Mrs. Craven went on. "I'll provide the quilt, the quilt frame, and all the supplies we need."

"Will we have to thread our own needles?" Sally Cook asked doubtfully. "I seem to spend more time threading my needle than sewing with it."

"So do I," said Christine Peacock.

"I'll thread your needle for you, Sally," said Bree, "and yours, too, Chris. I'll thread any needle that needs threading."

Mrs. Craven beamed at her. "Cooperation is the key to a pleasant and productive quilting bee. With many hands making light work, we may be able to finish the quilt in one day."

"What'll happen to it afterwards?" Bree asked.

"I thought we might use it as a raffle prize at the church fete," Mrs. Craven answered. "But I'm open to other ideas."

"I like the raffle idea," said Opal Taylor, and the rest of the Handmaidens nodded

25

their agreement. "Will you hold the quilting bee in your cottage, Mrs. Craven?"

"Don't be daft," said Mr. Barlow. "We'll hold it right here, in the schoolhouse. Only place for it."

He was right, of course. The villagers used the old schoolhouse for all sorts of communal activities — bottling jams, pickling vegetables, making sandwiches to sell at various events — because it was big enough, and it had enough empty floor space, to allow them to bustle about without bashing into one another.

"The schoolhouse would be ideal," said Mrs. Craven. "If you would assist me, Mr. Barlow —"

"At your service, ma'am," Mr. Barlow piped up readily.

"Thank you," said Mrs. Craven, nodding at him. "With your help, I'll have everything ready to go when the quilters arrive."

"The quilters," Elspeth Binney echoed happily. "It has a nice ring to it, doesn't it?"

"We'll work in shifts and we'll take as many breaks as we need," Mrs. Craven promised. "Otherwise we'll end up with stiff necks and sore fingers." She peered hesitantly at Peggy as she added, "If we might use the tea urn —"

"You leave the food and drink to us, dear,"

called Sally Cook. "We'll make sure there's plenty of both."

"When do you plan to hold this quilting bee of yours?" Peggy thundered.

Mrs. Craven took a deep breath and clasped her capable hands together tightly, as though bracing herself to deliver the most difficult part of her presentation.

"I thought we might hold it on Saturday," she said.

"On Saturday," Peggy repeated, looking confused. "Do you mean the day after tomorrow?"

"It's frightfully short notice, I know," said Mrs. Craven, "but I checked the schedule and Saturday is the only day the schoolhouse will be free until October."

There was a long pause. Brows furrowed, feet shuffled, and the energy that had filled the room began to dissipate. Mrs. Craven gave a soft sigh. I could almost hear her pet project sliding gently down the drain.

"Count me in," I declared, jumping to my feet. "Bess and I had planned to visit the stables on Saturday, but we can go there anytime. Your quilting bee will be really special, Mrs. Craven, a historic event I'll remember for the rest of my life. Every time I think of the quilt, I'll know I had a hand in creating a unique and beautiful heirloom that will be passed down from one generation to the next. I wouldn't miss your quilting bee for the world, Mrs. Craven. I'll be there!"

"Me, too," Bree said staunchly.

"And me," said Sally Cook. She tilted her head toward her husband. "I can leave Henry in charge of the tearoom."

"And I can leave Dick to run the pub," said Christine Peacock.

"I may pop in from time to time," bellowed Peggy Taxman, "but I won't be able to leave the Emporium for an entire day." She looked from Sally to Christine as she added haughtily, "Jasper and I work as a *team.*"

Sally and Christine let the barbed comment bounce off of them, while the rest of us tried, with varying degrees of success, to conceal our elation. Although our esteemed chairwoman was good at giving orders, she wasn't very good at taking them, especially when they came from someone as modest and soft-spoken as Mrs. Craven. With the possible exception of Jasper Taxman, everyone in the schoolhouse agreed, albeit silently, that the less time Peggy spent at the quilting bee, the more enjoyable it would be.

"You'll be most welcome whenever you

can join us," Mrs. Craven said to Peggy. "I might add that no one need stay for the entire day. You can drop in when you like and leave when you like."

"I'll be there for the duration," said Charles Bellingham. "It'll be like taking a master class in needlework."

"We'll be there, too," said Elspeth Binney, speaking on behalf of the Handmaidens. "We can go to the Saturday sales in Upper Deeping next week."

As the chorus of volunteers continued to swell, Mrs. Craven's gray eyes began to glisten. She lifted her clasped hands to her bosom and smiled tremulously, but she was clearly too moved to speak.

Peggy Taxman had no such trouble.

"Order!" she shouted, and when the hubbub subsided, she continued, "A quilting bee will be held in the schoolhouse on Saturday, starting at . . ." She paused to gaze inquisitively at Mrs. Craven.

"N-nine o'clock?" Mrs. Craven stammered, as if she couldn't quite believe that the tide had turned so overwhelmingly in her favor.

"Starting at nine o'clock in the morning," Peggy boomed. She pulled a blank sheet of paper from her official chairwoman's clipboard — which she also used for stocktaking at the Emporium — and scribbled a heading on it, then waved it in the air. "If you intend to participate in Mrs. Craven's quilting bee, add your name to the sign-up sheet." She dropped the sheet of paper on the long table and, with another stupendous bang of the gavel, adjourned the village affairs committee meeting for a second time.

While the others rushed forward to sign Peggy's improvised sign-up sheet, Mr. Barlow returned Bess to me and strolled over to confer with Mrs. Craven. Bree stood to avoid being trampled, then sat on the folding chair next to mine.

"Great speech, Lori," she said. "You saved the day."

"I had to," I said. "Your great-grandaunts would have come back to haunt me if I'd let Mrs. Craven down."

"They would have haunted all of us if we'd let her down," said Bree. "And we would have deserved it." She gazed at Mrs. Craven and mused aloud, "I wonder what kind of quilt it will be?"

"Knowing Finch as I do," I said, "it'll probably be a crazy quilt."

Bree laughed and I laughed along with her, little knowing that the quilt we would finish on Saturday would be Mrs. Craven's last gift to the village.

THREE

Saturday dawned fair and clear, with a slight nip in the air to remind me that it was still early April. As I rolled out of bed, I hoped Bill and the boys were enjoying similarly benign conditions, but a glance at the weather report suggested otherwise.

Although Bill had called several times to update me on his father-and-sons camping adventure, the cell phone connection had been so weak and wavering that I'd barely understood a word he'd said. I was fairly sure that he and the boys had spotted an osprey, but it was equally possible that he'd forgotten to bring the bug spray. Either way, he'd left me with the general impression that a good time was being had by all.

After an early breakfast, I placed Bess in her playpen and left her to entertain herself while I loaded our canary-yellow Range Rover with everything we'd need for our big day out: diaper bag, toy bag, insulated food bag, portable playpen to keep her from impaling herself on stray pins and needles while I worked on Mrs. Craven's quilt, and a plastic storage container filled with the butterscotch brownies I'd baked the night before. I knew that my plain-Jane brownies wouldn't hold a candle to the elaborate pastries my neighbors would bring to the quilting bee, but I also knew that Mr. Barlow was partial to them and I thought he deserved a reward for giving Mrs. Craven a helping hand.

At half past eight, I fetched Bess from the playpen, zipped her into a warm jacket, and gave her a purple plush stegosaurus to play with while I fastened the harness in her car seat. Job done, I climbed into the driver's seat, backed the Rover out of our graveled drive, and headed for the village.

I didn't need a calendar to tell me that spring had arrived in my little corner of the Cotswolds. All I had to do was to look around. A froth of may blossoms brightened the hedgerows that lined the narrow, winding lane, and primroses graced the verges. Lambs gamboled beside their grazing mothers in the hill pastures, and nesting birds flew hither and yon, long grasses trailing from their beaks.

We cruised past the mouth of the curving

drive that led to Anscombe Manor, where my best friend, Emma Harris, lived and where my sons' ponies, Thunder and Storm, were stabled. Emma ran a riding school, and since her Saturday classes were always booked solid, she'd been forced to decline her invitation to the quilting bee.

"Which is a pity," I said to Bess, "because Auntie Emma loves handicrafts almost as much as she loves horses."

"Horse!" Bess exclaimed.

I glanced fleetingly at Bree Pym's driveway as I negotiated the sharp curve in front of her mellow redbrick house. The absence of her secondhand sedan suggested that she'd left home early to assist Mr. Barlow as he implemented Mrs. Craven's plans.

Bess crowed with delight as we passed the wrought-iron gates that guarded the entrance to her grandfather's estate. She adored Willis, Sr., who regarded it as his sworn duty to indulge his only granddaughter's every whim. Though Grandpa William would spend the day reading, napping, and tending his orchids at Fairworth House, Grandma Amelia would be at the bee, sketchbook in hand, to record the historic event for posterity.

When we reached the top of the humpbacked bridge that crossed the Little Deeping River, I paused, as I always did, to savor the view. It was a view that never failed to warm my heart. The village lay before me, its golden buildings aglow in the morning light. Dew glistened on the elongated oval of tussocky grass that formed the village green, and the worn stones in the cobbled lane gleamed as if they'd been polished. St. George's stumpy bell tower peered shyly at me through the boughs of the churchyard's towering cedars, and the river rushed below me, rendered livelier than usual by spring rains.

A line of cars parked along the green indicated that word of the quilting bee had spread beyond the village to the farms that dotted the surrounding countryside. I was pleased to see the familiar vehicles because, while Finch was devoid of children, the farm families had plenty of them.

"The Hodges, the Malverns, and the Sciaparellis are here," I said to Bess. "It looks as though you'll have playmates your own age to keep you occupied while Mummy is otherwise engaged."

"Go!" Bess commanded.

I couldn't blame her for wanting to move on. Since she was facing backward, her view wasn't as appealing as mine.

Smiling, I left the bridge, bumped across

the cobbles, and parked in front of the tearoom. Henry Cook waved to me through the tearoom's wide front window, then hurried out to take the diaper bag, the toy bag, the insulated food bag, and the box of butterscotch brownies from me. When I reached for the portable playpen, however, he stopped me.

"You won't need it," he said. "Bree rigged up a baby jail — her word, not mine — to keep the little ones out of trouble. It already has a few inmates, but there's room for more."

"Excellent." I released Bess from her car seat, hoisted her and her stegosaurus into my arms, and closed the car door with my knee. "We're not late, are we?"

"It depends on what you mean by late," Henry replied. "Billy Barlow opened the schoolhouse for Mrs. Craven at six, Bree showed up ten minutes later, and the others started trickling in around eight."

"How many others?" I asked, opening the schoolhouse door.

"A fair few," said Henry. "Mrs. Craven's tickled pink by the turnout. I don't know why she waited so long to hold a quilting bee. She's having the time of her life."

A muffled buzz of conversation met my ears as I followed Henry into the cloakroom.

He deposited my bags and the box of brownies on a nearby bench, but the cloakroom was so crammed with coats, hats, and scarves that it took me a few minutes to find hooks for my jacket and Bess's.

"I'd best get back," said Henry. "I'm running the tearoom solo today. Sally'll have my head if I neglect our customers. Not that I'll have any to neglect." He cocked his head toward the schoolroom. "They're all in there."

"Sounds like it," I said. "Thanks for helping me with the heavy lifting."

"It was my pleasure." Henry stroked Bess's rosy cheek with his knuckles and left the schoolhouse, closing the front door behind him.

"Here we go," I said to Bess, and opened the door to the schoolroom.

In an instant, the muffled buzz became an unfiltered clamor of cheerful chatter. Nearly thirty women and precisely two men had descended on the schoolhouse, and all of them seemed to be talking at once, which was no mean feat, since most of them were also eating and drinking.

Despite the late notice, my neighbors had done their level best to make sure that no one who attended the quilting bee would go home hungry. The trestle tables that lined the wall to my left creaked beneath the weight of sausage rolls, savory scones, cheese straws, meat pies, canapés, quiches, and tall stacks of crustless sandwiches, while the tables to my right held enough pastries to stock a London bakery. The communal tea urn sat on a small table in front of the glass display cabinet that housed Finch's museum of odds and ends, and a table next to it held cups, saucers, cutlery, plates, and a pile of cloth napkins.

Mr. Barlow and Bree Pym stood at the front of the room, admiring Bree's handiwork. Bree's "baby jail" consisted of three playpens that had been taken apart and put together again to form one large, protected play area on the dais. Ten-year-old Maria Sciaparelli appeared to be the chief warden. She sat cross-legged in the middle of the merged playpens, ready to intervene if war broke out between her baby sister, her youngest cousin, and little Horace Malvern III.

Mrs. Craven flitted back and forth between two groups of seated women, who were evidently practicing the running stitch on layers of fabric sandwiched together in oversized embroidery hoops. A folding table between the two groups held a dozen more hoops as well as a clear plastic box filled with sewing supplies — scissors, thread, needles, thimbles, and several pairs of magnifying eyeglasses for those who'd forgotten to bring their reading glasses.

The main event was taking place in the center of the room.

Mrs. Craven's quilt frame resembled a long, narrow wooden table with trestle legs at either end and a quilt for a tabletop. The quilt had been rolled snugly around the side rails to keep it from sagging in the center, and a floor lamp stood at each end to provide extra light for the quilters, eight of whom were already hard at work.

The four Handmaidens sat in a row on one side of the frame, facing Charles Bellingham, Donna Sciaparelli, Annie Hodge, and Monica Malvern, who sat on the other side. Their needles flashed as they followed the simple stitching design Mrs. Craven had drawn on the quilt, but the task at hand didn't keep them from talking a mile a minute.

The quilt was a stunner. I couldn't put a name to the pattern, but it looked like an exploding star. Hundreds, if not thousands, of diamond-shaped bits of fabric had been sewn in concentric circles that seemed to expand outward from the eight-pointed star at their heart. The colors — indigo, ocher, crimson, sky-blue — were as dazzling as the pattern. I had no doubt whatsoever that Mrs. Craven's neglected masterpiece would raise a ton of money for St. George's Church, once it was finished.

Bess dropped her stegosaurus and began to babble excitedly. I lifted my gaze from the quilt to see Grandma Amelia approaching, her arms outstretched.

"There's my little darling," she said, taking Bess from me. "Aren't you the most beautiful girl in the world? Yes, you are! And the cleverest! And the strongest! And the sweetest! And . . ."

Amelia's paean to her step-granddaughter continued while I bent to retrieve the discarded dinosaur, but when I straightened, she turned her attention to me.

"Spectacular, isn't it?" she said, nodding at the quilt in the center of the room.

"There's no other word for it," I agreed.

"Mrs. Craven drew the stitching pattern on it with an air-soluble pencil," Amelia informed me. "In time, the lines will simply disappear. I didn't know such a thing existed."

"Nor did I," I said. "But the number of things I don't know about quilting would fill an encyclopedia."

"The frame's Victorian," Amelia went on. "Mr. Barlow tells me that it has pegged mortise-and-tenon joints and hand-cut ratchets, pawl gears, and teeth — the last three are the bits that make the rollers roll."

"What a treasure," I said. "It's bigger than I expected."

"The rollers are ninety-two inches long," said Lilian Bunting, crossing to join Amelia, Bess, and me. "It must have been made for someone with a spare barn or a very large house."

"Do you know what the quilt pattern is called?" I asked.

"Star of Bethlehem," Lilian replied, smiling. "Teddy was over the moon when Mrs. Craven told him. He thinks it's the perfect pattern for a church fund-raiser."

"How long have they been at it?" I asked, gesturing to the quilters seated at the frame.

"Not long," said Amelia. "Mrs. Craven won't let anyone work for more than thirty minutes. She says it'll keep us fresher. I say it'll keep us from becoming hunchbacks."

"Go!" Bess demanded, squirming impatiently.

Amelia lowered her to the floor and gave her two fingers to hold while we walked at a toddler's pace toward the baby jail. Mrs. Craven looked up at the sound of Bess's voice and left her stitchery class to walk with us.

"Here you are at last, Lori," she said, patting me on the arm. "As you can see, we started ahead of schedule."

"Your students are eager to learn," I told her. "As am I. I'll grab a hoop after I clap Bess behind bars."

"Bree's baby jail is a marvel," Mrs. Craven said admiringly. "Such a clever way to keep the little ones safe."

"Safe and busy," I amended. "There are few creatures on earth more destructive than a bored toddler, but Bess will have sparkling companions to amuse her while she's in the slammer."

"She'll have a surfeit of toys as well," Lilian commented. "It looks as though Monica Malvern brought Horace the Third's entire toy box with her."

"Maria's doling them out slowly," said Bree as we approached, "to make them last longer. She's an ideal jailer."

"I'll give her Bess's bag of toys to keep in reserve," I said. "Better to have too many than too few."

"Another inmate!" Bree announced as she scooped Bess up and placed her inside the linked playpens. "Keep an eye on this one, Maria. She's already hatching an escape plan."

Maria grinned, reached for the stegosaurus I held out to her, and used it to lure Bess to the rear of the enclosure, where the rest of the little prisoners were happily stacking wooden blocks, then knocking them over.

"You may think your baby jail's a joke," Lilian said to Bree, "but it's strangely appropriate to the setting. In Victorian prisons, convicts were put to work sewing mailbags."

"I can think of worse ways to spend time in prison," said Bree.

"So can I," said Amelia. "I'd prefer drawing to sewing, of course. Prison life would be almost bearable if I could sketch portraits of the other prisoners. I imagine they'd have very interesting faces."

"Interesting stories to tell, too," Bree put in.

"The only thing that would reconcile me to a jail sentence," I declared, "would be a guaranteed supply of Sally Cook's jam doughnuts."

"You needn't go to prison to enjoy Sally's doughnuts," said Lilian. "You'll find a rather large tray of them tucked between Opal Taylor's Bakewell tarts and my lemon bars."

"Bakewell tarts, lemon bars, *and* jam doughnuts?" I exclaimed. "I *love* quilting bees!"

"Let's hope you feel the same way by the

end of the day," said Mrs. Craven, chuck-ling.

I naively assured her that I would.

FOUR

Lilian sat between Amelia and Bree in our quilting class, but she merely listened while the rest of us discussed the pub's repainted sign, the selection of breakfast cereals at the Emporium, and various other hot topics. While the vicar's wife liked to keep abreast of the latest gossip, she wisely refrained from contributing to it in public.

Her husband showed up at half past nine to bless our endeavors. Everyone stood as the vicar delivered the uncharacteristically brief homily he'd composed especially for the occasion.

"Quilts, like friendships, bring warmth and comfort to our lives," he said. "May the Lord guide your needles and may the stitches you sew be as strong as the bonds of neighborly affection that unite our village. Amen."

He then took a seat at the quilt frame and executed a single workmanlike stitch.

"Impressive," I murmured to Lilian.

"He's been practicing since Thursday," she murmured back.

"I'll quit while I'm ahead, shall I?" said the vicar, standing.

His industriousness was rewarded with a round of applause, a cup of tea, and one of his wife's heavenly lemon bars.

The rest of the morning passed in a nearsighted blur. With Mrs. Craven's help, I learned how to hide my knots in the batting; how to catch all three layers of cloth with my needle; and how to sew a quick succession of stitches by rocking my needle up and down through the fabric several times before pulling the thread through.

The hardest lesson I had to learn was to relax.

"If you're tense, you'll end up with sore shoulders, a stiff neck, and a headache," Mrs. Craven told me. "We're not prisoners sewing mailbags, Lori. We're neighbors enjoying a pleasant pastime. Make knots in your thread, my dear, not in your muscles."

My first stitches could not have been mistaken for a robot's. They were distinctly human, and if it hadn't been for Mrs. Craven's leather thimbles, I would have left a trail of bloodstains on the fabrics sandwiched in my embroidery hoop. My technique improved with practice, however, and by the time I took a seat at the quilt frame, I'd achieved a level of competence that allowed me to chat, sew, and keep an eye on Bess without skewering myself or anyone else within reach of my needle.

When we finished one section of the quilt, Mr. Barlow turned the rollers to expose a new section and we began again. Mrs. Craven set an old-fashioned egg timer to ring at the end of our thirty-minute shifts. My first session felt like a life sentence, but the more I relaxed, the more quickly the minutes ticked by.

A midmorning shift change was in progress when Peggy Taxman barreled into the schoolhouse, claimed a seat at the frame, and astonished us all by demonstrating hitherto hidden quilting skills. Her needle seemed to dance across the colorful diamonds, and her stitches were indistinguishable from Mrs. Craven's.

"Don't look so surprised," she bellowed.

Startled, little Horace the Third burst into tears, but Bess burst into a gale of giggles. She thought Peggy Taxman was hilarious.

"My gran taught me how to quilt," Peggy continued. "It's like riding a bicycle — once learned, never forgotten. But I mustn't stay all day. I'll complete this section, then be on my way."

Peggy was as good as her thunderous word. The rest of us watched in awe as she moved from chair to chair, quilting like a woman possessed. When she was done, she waved off a cup of tea, declaring that she didn't have time to spare for such frivolities, and headed back to the Emporium.

"Will wonders never cease?" I said to Mrs. Craven.

"Quilting can be addictive," she observed. "The longer you've been away from it, the stronger its pull on you. If you're not careful, Lori, you'll find yourself falling under its spell."

"I'm pretty sure I've already fallen," I assured her, and it was true. By my third shift, quilting had begun to feel like a form of meditation. When I mentioned its calming effects to Lilian, she nodded.

"It would explain why Mrs. Craven is such a gentle soul," she said. "Her craft is a source of inner peace."

"Maybe we should buy a quilt frame for Peggy," I muttered, and Lilian suppressed a snort of laughter.

The other mothers disappeared with their sleepy babies and a flagging Maria around one o'clock, but after a hearty lunch, a stroll around the village green, and a nap on the baby jail's cushioned floor, Bess was raring to go. Thankfully, Bree volunteered to be her cell mate. Bree, who found quilting every bit as exciting as watching paint dry, was more than happy to exchange needles, thimbles, and thread for storybooks, plush dinosaurs, and games of Big Bad Bear on the green.

As the afternoon wore on, quilting fatigue began to take its toll. Sally Cook, Christine Peacock, Felicity Hobson, and Charles Bellingham were the first to abandon the bee. Amelia and Lilian departed a short time later, and the villagers who remained began to spend more time sipping tea and nibbling canapés than sewing. While they exchanged views on Opal Taylor's begonias, Selena Buxton's foray into the world of ballroom dancing, and Elspeth Binney's switch from oil to watercolor painting, Mrs. Craven and I soldiered on, sitting across from one another at the quilt frame.

When I pointed out to my companion that she and I were the only quilters who were actually working on the quilt, she smiled and told me not to worry.

"Haven't you noticed, my dear?" she said. "We're nearly done."

"Are we?" I said, flexing my tired fingers.

"We certainly are," said Mrs. Craven. "I

estimate that we have two square feet of quilting left to do. I'll have to bind the edges, of course, but I can easily do that on my own."

"I believe you could sew the clouds together and make a quilt in the sky," I told her.

"I'd need a bigger frame," she said with a self-deprecating chuckle.

"Where will you embroider your black-and-white cow?" I asked.

"It's a secret," she replied. "Will and Rob will have fun finding it."

"They always do," I said. "Did your mother teach you how to quilt?"

"My mother was a seamstress at the manor house in our village," said Mrs. Craven. "She taught me practical needlework. I learned to mend sheets, shirts, draperies, cushions — anything that could be sewn or woven. I taught myself to quilt much later, when I no longer had to earn a living with my needle."

Her casual reference to her old village piqued my curiosity. I'd stopped quizzing her about her former home years ago, after she'd explained that such questions brought back distressing memories of her husband's illness and death. By mentioning the place where her mother had worked, however, she seemed to indicate that the topic was no longer off limits.

I gave her a quick glance, then said cautiously, "You grew up in Old Cowerton, didn't you?"

"It was the only place I'd ever lived," she said, "until I came here."

"Is it like Finch?" I asked.

"It's larger than Finch," she said, "but smaller than Upper Deeping. Old Cowerton was an important crossroads in Tudor times. It went into a decline when the railway passed it by, but the motorcar rescued it. The tourist trade has kept Old Cowerton alive for as long as I can remember."

"I've seen the sign for Old Cowerton on the Oxford road," I said, "but I've never been there. It's not far from here, is it?"

"No more than thirty miles," she confirmed.

"Would you like to see it again, Mrs. Craven?" I asked. "If you would, I'll take you. We could make a day of it. Bess and I love to explore new places."

"You're very generous, my dear, but I have no desire to revisit my past," she said. "And please, Lori, call me Annabelle. You've known me far too long to address me as 'Mrs. Craven.' Besides, if we're to finish a quilt together, it's only right that you should use my Christian name."

"Thank you," I said, sewing with renewed vigor. Mrs. Craven hadn't invited anyone else in Finch to call her by her first name. I felt as if I'd been granted a singular privilege. "You're lucky to have such a pretty name, Annabelle."

"Do you think so?" she said. "It was a sore trial to me throughout my childhood. I should have been a Mildred or a Myrtle or a Mabel, but my mother wanted me to stand out from the other children, so I was christened Annabelle Beatrice." She shook her head and sighed. "You can imagine how well *that* went over in the school yard."

"I'm afraid I can," I said, smiling sympathetically. "Rob and Will get a kick out of calling their sister Messy Bessy. When she's older, I expect she'll call them Rob the Slob and Will the Pill. Children have a fairly basic sense of humor."

"Indeed, they do," Mrs. Craven agreed.

"Well, I think 'Annabelle Beatrice' is lovely," I said.

"Thank you." She sewed in silence for a moment, then said, "You didn't take your husband's surname when you married."

"No, I didn't," I said. "My husband is Bill Willis and our children are wee Willises, but

51

I was and always will be Lori Shepherd." I would have explained the reasoning behind my choice, but Mrs. Craven didn't require an explanation.

"Very sensible," she said. "I started life as Annabelle Greeley. I became Annabelle Trotter after I married my first husband, then Annabelle Craven after my second marriage. It was terribly inconvenient. With every name change, I had to replace all sorts of documents."

My inner busybody quivered with excitement, but I carried on as though my elderly neighbor hadn't provided me with the most riveting revelation I'd heard in months.

"I didn't know you were married twice," I said in a rigorously conversational tone of voice.

"Oh, yes," said Mrs. Craven. "My first husband was a man named Zachariah Trotter, though no one but his parents ever called him Zachariah. In the village, he was known as Zach."

"I've always liked the name Zachariah," I said.

"You wouldn't have liked Zach," she told me. "No one liked Zach."

"Why not?" I asked.

"He was a horrid man," Mrs. Craven replied dispassionately. "He was a drunk, a bully, a liar, and a cheat."

"I'm so sorry," I said, gazing at her with concern.

"Not as sorry as I was," she retorted. "But I wasn't sorry for long. We were married for less than a year."

"Did you divorce him?" I asked.

"Oh, no," she said, with a grim little smile. "I murdered him."

I laughed and looked around the room to see if anyone else had heard Mrs. Craven's outlandish joke, but Bree had taken Bess outside for a breath of fresh air and the others were too busy critiquing Christine Peacock's sausage rolls to eavesdrop on our conversation.

"I'm glad you're amused," said Mrs. Craven. "It was rather dreadful at the time, but I got over it much more quickly than I thought I would."

"Annabelle," I said, with the ghost of a smile still hovering on my lips, "you don't expect me to believe that you, of all people —"

"No one believed that I could be a cold-blooded killer," she interrupted. "Why would they? I didn't look like a hardened criminal and I certainly didn't behave like one. I was a tiny little thing, as pretty as a picture and as demure as a doe." She gave a satisfied nod. "My disguise was flawless."

I sat frozen with my needle in the air while Mrs. Craven continued to sew stitch after perfect stitch, seemingly unaware of the gravity of her confession. I studied her wrinkled hands and her white hair and thought sadly that her razor-sharp mind had finally lost its edge.

"Are you telling me a . . . a story?" I asked gently. "Something you read in a book or saw on television?"

"I am telling you a story," she acknowledged, "but it's a true story."

Stymied, I tried again.

"Annabelle," I said carefully, "are you taking any medications?"

"I'm not gaga, if that's what you're suggesting," she said, her gray eyes twinkling. "Doctor Finisterre will confirm that I'm in full possession of my faculties. I only wish I'd been as clearheaded when I was seventeen. If I'd refused Zach's proposal in the first place, I could have avoided the whole messy business."

"M-messy business?" I faltered, as visions of chain saws danced in my head.

"My marriage was the messy business," she clarified. "The murder was really quite tidy."

"Was it?" I said faintly.

"Oh, yes," she said. "Zach was drunk, you see. One little push was enough to send him tumbling down the stairs in our cottage. I'm almost certain that the fall broke his neck. His head was bent at *such* an odd angle."

I was vaguely aware of Bree reentering the schoolhouse with Bess in her arms, but I didn't look up or smile at them. I couldn't take my eyes off of Mrs. Craven, who'd tilted her head to one side, as if to illustrate her husband's fatal injury.

"To be absolutely certain, I gave Zach a tap on the head with the poker," she went on. "Luckily, he didn't bleed. Bloodstains would have complicated matters considerably." She frowned thoughtfully. "They're very difficult to remove from floorboards."

"Are they?" I asked weakly.

"Yes, indeed," she answered. "I'd practiced with chickens."

My jaw dropped.

"I learned the true meaning of deadweight that night," she went on. "But where there's a will, there's a way! I rolled Zach onto a rug, dragged him into the garden, and buried him in the trench I'd dug for my rosebushes. I planted the roses early the next morning and that was that." She paused to snip her thread, then smiled broadly. "I must say that Zach's decaying corpse did wonders for my roses. I thought a dead body would enrich the soil and I was right."

I winced and turned away from her as my scrambled brain struggled to reconcile the woman who fed my sons shortbread cookies with the woman who'd fed her husband to the worms.

"Was . . . was Zach cruel to you?" I asked. "Did you kill him in self-defense?"

"Zach never raised a hand to me," she said. "I was embarrassed by him rather than terrified of him. In the end, I simply wanted to be rid of him."

"You could have divorced him," I pointed out with some asperity.

"I couldn't afford the legal fees," she said. "As you can imagine, Zach wasn't a reliable breadwinner. We could scarcely afford to pay our bills." She smiled serenely. "Take it from me, Lori: Divorces are expensive. Murder is cheap."

"Annabelle!" I cried, horrified. When several heads swiveled in my direction, I bent over the quilt and lowered my voice. "Didn't anyone notice that Zach was missing?"

"Everyone noticed," she said, "including the nice young constable who came to call on me a few days later. I told him tearfully that Zach had abandoned me. I had no trouble convincing him. Zach was so very unlikable, you see, and I was the personification of injured innocence. The constable very kindly helped me to file a missing person report. Seven years later, Zach was declared dead and I was free to marry again. Needless to say, I was more selective the second time around."

"Did you tell your second husband what you'd done?" I asked.

"Certainly not," she said, gazing at me incredulously. "I don't think he'd have married me if he'd known that I'd killed my first husband, do you?"

"If you didn't tell *him*," I said in an urgent whisper, "why are you telling *me*?"

"Oh, I just thought you might find it interesting," she said. She took my needle from my unresisting hand, completed my stitch, and sat back in her chair. "There. It's finished. Come and see, everyone! Lori and I have finished the quilt!"

While the others gathered around to congratulate Mrs. Craven — and themselves — on a job well done, I rose from my chair, backed away from the quilt frame, and turned to lift Bess from the baby jail.

"We're free!" Bree shouted, flinging her

arms wide. "Thanks, Bess. That was the most fun I've ever had in prison."

"Good to hear," I said distractedly. "Tell Mr. Barlow he can have the rest of the butterscotch brownies."

I crossed to the cloakroom, feeling as though someone had tapped me on the head with a poker. I donned my jacket and helped Bess into hers, then carried her to the Range Rover, secured her in her safety seat, and drove home without pausing to savor any views. I was desperate to confide in someone who would help me to make sense of something that made no sense at all.

I needed to speak with Aunt Dimity.

FIVE

No more than a scant handful of people knew about my friendship with Aunt Dimity. I wasn't ashamed of her. Indeed, I loved her with all my heart. She was simply very difficult to explain.

Dimity Westwood, an Englishwoman, had been my late mother's closest friend. The two women had met in London while serving their respective countries during the Second World War. The experiences they shared during those dark and dangerous times created a bond between them that was never broken.

When the war in Europe ended and my mother sailed back to the States, she and Dimity continued to share their everyday lives by sending hundreds of letters back and forth across the Atlantic. After my father's sudden death, those letters became my mother's refuge, a peaceful retreat from the daily grind of working full time as a schoolteacher while raising a rambunctious daughter on her own.

My mother was extremely protective of her refuge. She told no one about it, not even me. As a child, I knew Dimity Westwood only as Aunt Dimity, the redoubtable heroine of a series of bedtime stories that sprang from my mother's fertile imagination — or so I thought. I didn't learn until much later that her stories were inspired by her dear friend's letters. I knew nothing about the real Dimity Westwood until after both she and my mother had died.

It was then that Dimity Westwood bequeathed to me a comfortable fortune, the honey-colored cottage in which she'd spent her childhood, her precious postwar correspondence with my mother, and a curious blue leather–bound book filled with blank pages. It was through the blue journal that I first met my benefactress.

Whenever I opened the blue journal, Aunt Dimity's handwriting would appear, an old-fashioned copperplate taught in the village school at a time when home births were the rule, not the exception. I thought I'd lost my mind the first time it happened, but a second line of graceful script, followed by a third, finally convinced me that Aunt Dimity wasn't a bizarre hallucination. She was a kindly soul whose intentions were wholly benevolent.

I couldn't explain how Aunt Dimity managed to bridge the gap between life and afterlife — and she wasn't too clear about it, either — but I didn't much care. The important thing, the only thing that mattered, was that Aunt Dimity was as good a friend to me as she'd been to my mother. The rest was mere mechanics.

Bess's eyelids began to droop as we crossed the humpbacked bridge. By the time I pulled into our graveled drive, she was sound asleep. Instead of waking her, I carried her into the cottage and straight upstairs to the nursery. My daughter was a distressingly fearless ball of energy, but a full day of nonstop socializing was a lot to expect from any toddler. I knew that an early night would do her more good than harm.

Bess grumbled vaguely while I got her ready for bed, but she dropped off as soon as I lowered her into the crib. I switched on the baby monitor, clipped the mobile receiver to a belt loop on my jeans, and made my way back downstairs, where I was waylaid by Stanley, who made it abundantly clear that he was ready for his dinner. I apologized for the delay and followed him into the kitchen to fill his food bowl, freshen his water bowl, and assure him that Bill — his favorite human — would be home before he knew it. Only then was I free to do what I'd longed to do ever since I'd backed away from the quilt frame.

I let myself into the study.

The study, unlike the schoolhouse, was still and silent. A brisk breeze ruffled the strands of ivy that covered the diamond-paned windows above the old oak desk, but the chill that gripped me had nothing to do with the crisp evening air. I lit the mantel lamps and knelt to light a fire in the hearth, then stood to make a shocking announcement to my oldest friend in the world.

"Reginald," I said. "I think I may have spent the day sewing with a psychopath."

Reginald was a small powder-pink flannel rabbit. He'd entered my life on the day I'd entered it and he'd been by my side ever since. A sensible woman would have put him away when she put away childish things, but I wasn't a sensible woman. Instead of wrapping my bunny in tissue and sticking him in a drawer, I kept him in a special niche in the study's floor-to-ceiling bookshelves, where I could commune with him whenever the need arose.

"I'm not kidding," I added somberly.

I wasn't completely crazy. I knew that my pink flannel bunny couldn't speak. But I could tell by the gleam in his black button eyes that I'd captured his attention. I nodded portentously, took the blue journal from its shelf, and sat with it in one of the tall leather armchairs that faced the hearth.

"Dimity?" I said as I opened the journal. "I just had the *strangest* conversation with old Mrs. Craven."

Good evening, Lori. I presume your conversation took place at the quilting bee. Was the bee a success?

"We finished quilting the quilt," I said, "and everyone seemed to have a good time, but right at the end of it, when Mrs. Craven and I were alone at the quilt frame, she" — I hesitated, then plunged on regardless — "she told me that she murdered her first husband."

I beg your pardon?

"I know," I said, nodding vigorously. "It's nuts, isn't it?"

Did you believe her?

"Not at first," I replied. "At first I thought she was telling a weird joke. When I realized that she meant what she said, I told myself that old age had finally caught up with her. Delusions seem to go hand in hand with dementia."

Did she seem demented?

"No," I said. "She didn't cackle maniacally or behave like a zombie. As far as I could tell, she was her usual self."

I wouldn't expect someone like Mrs. Craven to harbor violent delusions, even if her mind was slipping. Did she describe the murder?

"She gave me every gory detail," I said. "She told me how she killed him, what she did with his body, and how she fooled a nice young constable into believing her cover story."

Can you tell me exactly what she said?

"Oh, yes," I said. "It's not the sort of thing I'll forget in a hurry." I leaned back in my chair, kicked off my shoes, propped my stockinged feet on the ottoman, and repeated Mrs. Craven's account of the murder and its aftermath. When I finished, I shook my head again. "She didn't seem to think it was a big deal, Dimity. She wasn't melodramatic or sinister. She just nattered on matter-of-factly, as if we were discussing a bag of buttons she'd bought in Upper Deeping."

And she expressed no guilt or remorse?

"None," I said. "If anything, she was proud of herself for being so clever. The whole thing was completely absurd, and yet . . ." My voice trailed off as I raised a helpless hand, then let it fall.

And yet you believed her.

"I sort of did," I admitted. "That's the problem. If she really did kill her husband, won't I have to turn her in to the police? I mean, it's the sort of thing an upright citizen is supposed to do, isn't it?" I lifted my gaze and stared bleakly into the fire. "Can you imagine me ratting out Mrs. Craven? The police would think *I'm* nuts, and the villagers would write me off as a heartless monster, especially if she isn't quite as compos mentis as we'd all like to believe she is." I sighed miserably and looked down at the journal. "I'd have to be very sure of my facts before I took such a drastic step."

Have you told Bill about Mrs. Craven's confession?

"Not yet," I said. "I haven't spoken with him since last night, and even then I couldn't hear half of what he said. His campsite seems to be in a cell phone dead spot."

In that case, it would be foolish to relay Mrs. Craven's disturbing story to him. The chances for misunderstanding are too great. He might rush home, expecting to find Mrs. Craven standing over your lifeless body with a bloody poker.

"The connection is pretty lousy," I acknowledged. "I wouldn't want to frighten him."

Even if you could make yourself understood, I'd advise against it.

"Why?" I asked.

Your husband is an officer of the court, Lori. If he has knowledge of a crime, he's required by law to report it to the authorities. It would be unkind to disrupt his camping trip with an unconfirmed suspicion.

"I'd hate to spoil his holiday," I said slowly, "especially when he and the boys are having so much fun." I thought for a moment, then nodded decisively. "Point taken, Dimity. I'll keep my unconfirmed suspicion to myself until Bill and the boys come home."

You could, of course, become sure of your facts before *Bill and the boys come home.*

"How?" I asked.

For pity's sake, Lori, the answer is staring you in the face!

"Please don't ask me to think," I begged. "I've had an awfully long day."

Go to Old Cowerton, my dear. Spend some time there.

"And do what?" I asked.

You're a Finch-trained snoop, Lori. Use your incomparable investigative skills to verify or to debunk Mrs. Craven's story. Visit the scene of the alleged crime. Chat with the locals. If you're lucky, you'll find someone who knew Mrs. Craven when she was Mrs. Trotter — a neighbor, a friend, a schoolmate. Old Cowerton may be larger than Finch, but it's still a village. I'm sure that someone there knows what really happened to Zachariah Trotter.

"I'd have to bring Bess with me," I said doubtfully.

Forgive me, my dear, but you're stating the obvious. Bess may be advanced for her age, but she's not sufficiently advanced to change her own nappies.

"What I mean is, I can't leave her with William and Amelia," I said. "She already misses her daddy and her brothers. She'd be very upset if I went away as well."

I'm not asking you to abandon your child, Lori.

"I know, but it's not easy to travel with a toddler," I said. "You have no conception of how many things I'd have to pack. I might as well hook the cottage to the back of the Rover and drag it along with me."

On the plus side, people will be drawn to Bess. They always are. Her presence will make it easier for you to strike up conversations with strangers.

I lifted my gaze from the page and stared

into the fire. A day that had started so brightly had ended on a very dark note indeed. When I tried to imagine good-hearted, gentle Mrs. Craven standing over the body of a man she'd murdered in cold blood, I saw nothing but her hand moving calmly and steadily as she sewed stitch after perfect stitch. Was she a psychopath? Or was she delusional? I didn't know what to believe.

"Let me sleep on it," I said, rubbing my forehead as I looked down at the journal. "I'll make a decision in the morning."

I believe you've already made a decision.

"Have I?" I said.

Of course you have. You've decided to go to Old Cowerton, despite the difficulties such a trip will entail, because you're incurably curious. You won't be at peace with yourself until you know the truth about Mrs. Craven.

I smiled ruefully. Aunt Dimity knew me too well.

"You're probably right," I admitted, "but —" I broke off, interrupted by the doorbell.

A late caller?

"It's not late," I said, "but I clearly have a caller. I'd better find out who it is. I'll talk to you later, Dimity."

I doubt it. You'll be too busy packing.

I laughed as the fine lines of royal-blue

ink faded from the page, but when I thought of the task that lay before me, my laughter died.

My neighbors and I swapped gossip on a daily basis, but the tidbits we exchanged were essentially harmless. We might do a little digging to find out why someone wasn't speaking to someone else, but we didn't pry open closet doors, searching for skeletons.

I was about to embark on a search for an actual skeleton. If I found it, I would utterly ruin what little time Annabelle Craven had left on earth. What's more, I'd disrupt the peace of a place I held dear. When the villagers realized how grossly they'd misjudged Mrs. Craven, they might begin to have doubts about one another. Finch's timeless tranquillity would be tainted by suspicion and unease. The villagers might even begin to lock their doors.

Even so, I couldn't allow a murderer to live among my neighbors undetected. I didn't want to investigate Mrs. Craven, but I had no choice. In my universe, homicide wasn't an acceptable alternative to divorce. It was a crime without a statute of limitations.

"No happy camping for me," I said to Reginald as I returned the blue journal to its shelf. "I have a job to do."

My pink bunny's eyes glimmered with sympathy as I left the study to answer the front door.

Six

I opened the door to find Bree Pym standing on my doorstep, loaded down with Bess's diaper bag, toy bag, and insulated food bag.

"I found these in the cloakroom," she explained, patting the bags, "so I thought I'd bring them by."

"You're an angel," I said. "Come in. I'll put the kettle on."

Bree dropped two of the bags on the floor in the front hall and hung her jacket on the coatrack. She brought the food bag to the kitchen, emptied it, and washed it out before taking a seat at the kitchen table.

"I'd have been here sooner," she said, "but I stayed behind to help Mr. Barlow dismantle the quilt frame and clean up the schoolhouse. You should have seen his face when I told him he could take your butterscotch brownies home with him. I thought he was going to yodel."

I smiled but said nothing as I laid the table for tea. I wasn't in the mood for idle chatter. When the kettle whistled, I filled the pot, carried it to the table, and sat across from Bree, but my mind was thirty miles away, in a tourist town where a pretty young woman had gotten away with murder.

"It's not like you to forget your baby stuff, Lori," Bree observed. "It's not like you to leave a village event without saying goodbye to everyone. And it's definitely not like you to be so . . . mute."

"I guess I'm not myself this evening," I said with a wan attempt at humor.

"Why?" Bree asked, frowning worriedly. "Has something happened to Bill or the twins?"

"As far as I know, they're having tons of fun," I said.

"You must miss them," said Bree. "I'm used to Jack running off on his lecture tours, but the house still seems a bit empty without him."

"I'm not pining for Bill and the boys," I assured her. "I'm glad they're having a good time."

"You don't look glad," she said, studying my expression. "You look like a rat died under your bed." Her dark eyes widened. "Did a rat die under your bed?"

"Nothing died under my bed," I stated firmly.

"Then tell me what's wrong," she said.

"I'm fine, really," I told her. "And, anyway, you won't believe me."

"Of course I will," she said. "Come on, Lori, spit it out. I won't leave until you do. I'll dog your steps for the rest of the evening. I'll stand over your bed all night, staring down at you like a deranged ghost. I'll —"

"All right, all right," I broke in, knowing when I was beaten. "I'll tell you the whole story on one condition: You have to promise that you won't breathe a word of it to anyone — not even to Jack — until I give you the go-ahead. I mean it, Bree. What I'm about to tell you is *strictly* confidential."

"I'm not one of the Handmaidens," she reminded me. "I know how to keep my trap shut. I kept it shut when we were looking for the lost prince, didn't I?"

"Yes, you did," I said, recalling the strange journey Bree and I had shared less than a year after she'd moved to Finch. "To be honest, it'll be a relief to get it off my chest. It's just so weird. . . ."

"I love weird," Bree declared. "The weirder, the better. Bring it on."

"Okay," I said. "Brace yourself."

I filled her cup and mine, folded my hands

on the table, and for the second time in less than an hour, recounted Mrs. Craven's disturbing tale. By the time I finished, Bree was frowning so hard that her eyebrows nearly touched.

"Mrs. Craven? A stone-cold killer?" She shook her head. "I don't believe you."

"Told you so," I said wistfully.

"It's impossible," she said.

"It's improbable," I countered, "but it's not impossible."

"She's a sweet little old lady," Bree protested.

"She wasn't a sweet little old lady back then," I pointed out. "She was an unhappy teenager. Unhappy teenagers have been known to do terrible things."

"What does Bill think?" Bree demanded.

"I don't know," I said. "I haven't told him about the late Mr. Trotter and I don't intend to. Not yet, anyway."

"Why not?" she asked.

"As an attorney, he'd be required by law to take the story to the police," I explained, "and I don't want to involve the police until I figure out whether Mrs. Craven was telling the truth or indulging in wishful thinking or displaying symptoms of senility."

"How will you decide?" she asked. "Are you planning to strap Mrs. Craven to a lie detector?"

"No," I said. "Bess and I are going to spend a few days in Old Cowerton. If I can find someone who knew Mrs. Craven back then, I may be able to nail down a few facts."

"They may be unpleasant facts," Bree cautioned. "What'll you do if you find out that she really did kill her husband?"

"That's when I'll talk to Bill," I said.

Bree drained her cup, smacked her lips, and eyed me determinedly.

"Well," she said, "you and Bess aren't going to Old Cowerton alone. I'm coming with you."

I smiled. "Thanks, Bree, but I can't let you —"

"Try and stop me," she interrupted. "What kind of friend would I be if I sat at home while you and Bess did all the legwork?"

"You don't understand," I said. "I shouldn't be doing the legwork. The *police* should be doing the legwork. I should have gone straight to them with my story. If I find out that Mrs. Craven murdered her first husband, I could be accused of withholding information or aiding and abetting or being an accessory after the fact."

"Sounds serious," Bree said with mock solemnity.

"It *is* serious," I insisted. "I don't want you to get into trouble."

"Then you shouldn't have told me about Mrs. Craven," she pointed out.

"You gave me no choice!" I exclaimed.

"Get used to it," she said, "because you have no choice about whether I'm coming with you or not. You're stuck with me, Lori. If there's trouble to be faced, we'll face it together. Besides . . ." Her dark eyes twinkled mischievously as she leaned over her teacup and murmured, "I'm *dying* to see Mrs. Craven's rosebushes."

I snickered involuntarily and Bree grinned.

"It's not funny," I scolded.

"It's a little funny," she countered.

"All right," I admitted, "it's a little funny."

I gazed gratefully at Bree, feeling as if she'd lifted the weight of the world from my shoulders. If anyone could keep my spirits up during my bizarre investigation, I thought, she could.

"We'll need a cover story," she said, getting down to business. "How about: We're going on a girls-only getaway inspired by Bill's camping trip?"

"Works for me," I said. "I'll try it out on Amelia when I ask her to look after Stanley. We'll also need a place to stay in Old Cowerton — preferably a family-friendly place. I hate it when people give Bess the stink eye for doing what toddlers do."

"Family friendly, check," said Bree, as if she were making a mental list. "Cost?"

"Not an issue," I said, silently thanking Aunt Dimity. "And I'll foot the bill."

"No, you won't," she objected.

"Yes, I will," I told her.

"When the time comes, I'll arm-wrestle you for my half of it," she concluded. "How long will we be away?"

"I want to get back before Bill and the boys come home," I said. "If we leave tomorrow, we'll have" — I glanced at the wall calendar — "six full days at our disposal."

"In case you've forgotten, tomorrow's Sunday," said Bree. "We'll get plenty of stink eyes if we're not in church. And the vicar will probably cry."

"We'll go to the early service," I suggested.

"Good idea," she said, nodding. "Hardly anyone goes to the early service, so we won't be expected to spend an hour chatting in the churchyard afterward."

"I'll pick you up on the way to Finch," I said, "and we'll leave from St. George's."

"Right." Bree pulled her cell phone out of her pocket with a flourish and sat back in her chair. "I'll find a place to stay. If Old

Cowerton really is a tourist town, it shouldn't be too hard to make a reservation somewhere. Early April isn't the height of tourist season."

"It's Easter break, though," I said. "The town may be crawling with families."

"Leave it to me," she said.

While Bree tapped and swiped, I picked up the phone in the kitchen and dialed Amelia's number the old-fashioned way.

"Lori!" Amelia exclaimed upon hearing my voice. "What a pleasant coincidence. I was about to ring you for a final report on the quilting bee."

"The quilt's done," I informed her, "except for a few finishing touches Mrs. Craven can add on her own."

"Three cheers for Finch," she crowed. "That quilt will fetch an absolute fortune at the church fete."

"No doubt," I agreed, and pressed on. "I have a favor to ask of you, Amelia. Would you mind taking care of Stanley for a few days? Bree and I have decided to take Bess with us on a girls' getaway."

"Good for you," she said. "Why should the boys have all the fun? And, yes, of course I'll look after Stanley. You know how fond I am of him. When are you leaving?"

"Directly after church tomorrow," I said.

"I'm afraid Bess and I won't make it to Sunday brunch."

Sunday brunch was a family institution at Fairworth House. I regretted missing it, but I couldn't in good conscience delay our departure until dinnertime, which was when Willis, Sr.'s Sunday brunches usually ended.

"William will be disappointed," Amelia acknowledged, "but I'll break it to him gently. If the weather's fine, I might even persuade him to come with me to see the gardens at Hidcote. I've heard the daffodils are spectacular this year. Where are you going?"

"I'm not sure," I said with incomplete honesty. Though I knew we'd be in Old Cowerton, I didn't yet know where we'd stay. "But I'll bring my cell phone with me so we can keep in touch."

"Don't worry about keeping in touch," she said. "Don't worry about Stanley or the cottage or anything at all. Have a wonderful, worry-free holiday. We'll see you when you get back."

"Thank you, Amelia," I said. "I really appreciate it."

"Not at all," she said. "Remember to take lots of photos!"

"I will," I promised, but as I said goodbye, I had to stifle another morbid snicker.

What kind of photos, I wondered, did one take when engaged in a corpse hunt? I could only hope that Bree and I wouldn't end up posing for mug shots.

I hung up the phone and turned to find my young friend looking mightily pleased with herself.

"We're staying at the White Hart Hotel," she announced, "a historic, five-star hostelry centrally located on Old Cowerton's high street. The White Hart has a walled garden, a restaurant, a pub, twenty-four-hour room service, an indoor swimming pool, a spa —"

"It has a spa?" I interrupted.

"Wait," she told me. "It gets better."

"What's better than a spa?" I asked.

"A fully equipped, two-bedroom family suite," she answered. "I reserved a cot, a playpen, a high chair, and a changing table for Bess."

"I'll bring disinfectant," I said.

"Lori, it's a five-star hotel," Bree said patiently. "It wouldn't have five stars if it loaned disease-ridden baby furniture to its guests."

"I'll bring disinfectant," I repeated.

"Suit yourself," she said, shrugging. "The White Hart also offers the services of a board-certified nanny."

"We won't need a nanny," I said flatly.

"It's nice to have backup," said Bree. "There's no check-in time, by the way. Our suite will be ready for us whenever we arrive."

"How on earth did you manage to find a family suite in a tourist town during Easter break?" I asked.

"Charm," she replied, "and an excellent credit rating."

"Well done," I said, clapping her on the back. "If I weren't dreading our trip, I'd look forward to it."

The kitchen telephone rang. I answered it and heard my husband's voice broken into a series of truncated syllables that resembled Morse code. I couldn't understand more than a morsel of the fractured conversation that followed, but I did my best to convey our cover story to him before the call was abruptly cut off.

"Bill?" queried Bree.

"For all I know, it could have been the president of Peru," I said. "Cell phones are handy, but they'll never replace landlines. I'll call him from Old Cowerton. Maybe the reception will be better there. Are you hungry? I could scramble some eggs."

"Thanks," said Bree, "but Mr. Barlow and I polished off Christine Peacock's sausage rolls before we left the schoolhouse." She

81

stood. "I'm going home to pack."

"Oh, Lord," I groaned, putting a hand to my forehead. "I forgot about packing."

"Look on the bright side," said Bree. "You won't have to pack Bess's cot!"

"Thanks, Bree," I said. "Thanks for bringing Bess's bags home and for finding the perfect hotel and for reserving the baby furniture and for . . . for everything. I'll sleep much better tonight, knowing that you're coming with us."

"Don't be silly," she said lightly. "I should be thanking you. I've always wanted to be a gumshoe."

I walked her to the front door and waved her off, then ran upstairs to look in on Bess. She was still catching up on her beauty sleep, so I let her be and began the gargantuan task of assembling everything I would need for a six-day trip with a toddler.

After loading Bess's three-wheeled, all-terrain pram into the Range Rover and carrying several suitcases filled with baby gear downstairs, I grabbed my shoulder bag from the table in the front hall and went to the study.

"Reginald," I said, "Bess and I are taking a short and, I fear, necessary holiday with Bree Pym. Amelia will look after the cottage while we're gone, but I'm leaving you in charge of the study. If Bill calls, take a message."

I took my bunny from his special niche and gave him a hug, then put him back where he belonged and reached for the blue journal. I slipped the journal into my shoulder bag, but I didn't open it.

I was too busy packing.

Seven

Bree was standing by her gate when I stopped to pick her up on Sunday morning. Although she hadn't removed her nose ring, she'd transformed her spiky hairdo into a demure pixie cut and dressed in an unusually subdued manner, if a beige trench coat, a voluminous floral-print neck scarf, a kelly-green day pack, black jeans, navy socks, and violet clogs could be called subdued.

I heard her chuntering under her breath as she added her modest nylon carryall to the gear I'd stowed in the Range Rover's cargo compartment, but after she climbed into the passenger seat and said a cheery hello to Bess, she expressed herself with perfect clarity.

"Are you sure you remembered to bring everything?" she asked. "I didn't see a kitchen sink back there."

"You mock what you do not understand," I said loftily as I pulled into the lane.

"Babies need a lot of stuff."

"Obviously," Bree muttered, glancing over her shoulder.

"What's with the trench coat?" I asked. "And why did you change your hair?"

"It's my gumshoe disguise," she replied. "Private eyes are supposed to blend in with their surroundings."

"The clogs may give you away," I hinted.

"They're not inconspicuous," she conceded, studying her footwear, "but I thought they'd blend in better than my bumblebee Wellies."

I couldn't argue with her. Violet clogs were marginally less eye-catching than black-and-yellow-striped Wellington boots.

As Bree had predicted, the early service at St. George's was sparsely attended. Lilian and the vicar were clearly pleased to see us fill three empty spots in a pew. They greeted us with a mixture of warmth and genteel curiosity as we exited the church, but our cover story seemed to satisfy them and we were able to get away relatively quickly.

"Did you see the look on Lilian's face?" I asked as Finch receded in my rearview mirror. "I thought she was going to ask if she could come with us."

"It's a good thing she didn't," said Bree. "We don't have room for another suitcase."

I smiled serenely and murmured, "There's always the roof rack."

Thirty miles might not seem like a great distance in the United States, but in rural England, thirty miles often felt like sixty. Once we left the Oxford road, I found myself driving down a narrow, twisting lane not unlike the one that meandered picturesquely from my cottage to Finch. Sweeping views of the rolling countryside provided some compensation for our frustratingly slow progress until the lane descended into a shallow, bowl-shaped valley.

Old Cowerton lay at the bottom of the bowl, though a scattering of houses climbed up the sides. The town was, as Mrs. Craven had foretold, larger than Finch but smaller than Upper Deeping. A towering spire suggested that its church was much grander than St. George's, and I was willing to bet that the large, enclosed property on the far side of the valley belonged to the local manor house.

An outlying enclave of drab brown brick row houses heralded our approach to the town proper. Verdant pastures soon gave way to a rabbit warren of streets lined with golden limestone buildings that were every bit as venerable as Finch's, though there were more of them and they were more tightly packed together.

To judge by the number of parked cars protruding unapologetically into my lane, garages were nonexistent in Old Cowerton. I held my breath as I squeezed past oncoming vehicles and loosened my death grip on the steering wheel only when we entered the much wider high street.

A variety of shops, art galleries, cafés, and restaurants lined the high street, but the White Hart Hotel stood head and shoulders above them all. Four stories tall and four gabled bays across, it seemed massive compared to its less imposing neighbors. It would have dominated the scene unpleasantly if it hadn't been built with the same stone and in the same style as the rest of the high street's buildings. Unlike Bree's violet clogs, it blended in.

The White Hart was set back from the street, with a small courtyard tucked between the projecting end bays. The arrangement allowed me to park the Rover near the front of the hotel without risking a rear-end collision. I'd barely switched off the engine when two young porters emerged from an iron-banded oak door to escort Bree and me from the car to the courtyard, where we were met by an older man.

The older man was tall and thin and neatly dressed in a dark blue shirt and a double-breasted light gray suit. I thought he might be in his late thirties. He had fine lines around his deep-set blue eyes and he wore his wavy blond hair combed back from a receding hairline. His hands were impeccably manicured, his mauve tie matched his pocket square, and his black leather shoes were polished to perfection. He spoke softly but precisely, and his accent suggested a birthplace closer to Rome than to Old Cowerton.

"Madam Shepherd, Madam Pym," he said, bowing courteously to each of us, in the correct order. "Welcome to the White Hart. I am Francesco and I will be your personal concierge during your stay."

"How did you know —" I began, but Bree cut me off.

"I described you, me, Bess, and the Range Rover when I made the reservation," she explained.

"Your description was most helpful, madam," said Francesco.

"*Go!*" bellowed Bess, with the imperiousness of an infant Peggy Taxman.

"My daughter," I said to our personal concierge as I scurried back to the Rover, where the two young porters were entertaining Bess by making funny faces at her through the car window.

Francesco strode ahead of me to open the car door, then stood back while I retrieved my backseat bellower. Having taken her morning nap in the Rover, Bess was ready to run a marathon. I lowered her to the sidewalk, grabbed her hand to keep her from toddling headlong into the high street, and redirected her wobbly steps toward the courtyard.

"If you will give me your keys, madam," said Francesco, "Eric and Lazlo will attend to your luggage."

My keys were duly passed to the porters, who took possession of the Rover and disappeared with it up a cobbled alleyway beside the hotel.

"I'm afraid we have rather a lot of luggage," I said to Francesco, with an apologetic grimace.

"We?" said Bree, raising an eyebrow.

"Okay, most of it's mine," I admitted.

"Naturally," said Francesco. "My son, Frankie, he is small, like your daughter. When my wife and I travel, we fill the car to the roof. We pack more for Frankie than we do for ourselves."

I smirked at Bree, who lowered her eyebrow and avoided my gaze.

Francesco guided us across the small courtyard, through the iron-banded door, and into a low-ceilinged lobby with an uneven flagstone floor and timber-framed white plaster walls. Two ancient elevators lurked discreetly beneath an oak staircase lined with gilt-framed oil paintings of heroically proportioned horses, bulls, and pigs — suitable subjects, I thought, in a country town surrounded by lush farmland.

The hotel's front desk wasn't a bunker barricaded behind a bank of computers but a gleaming walnut table with graceful cabriole legs. A tablet computer was the lobby's only visible concession to the twenty-first century.

After helping us to remove our coats, Francesco handed them to Leah, the fresh-faced and well-dressed receptionist, then steered us past her.

"Don't we have to sign in?" I asked him.

"There is no need, madam," he replied. "It is taken care of." He handed each of us a key card, then drew a tiny cell phone from his breast pocket and presented it to me. "If you need anything, day or night, press *one* and I will answer. I am always at your service." He clasped his hands together and continued energetically, "With your permission, I will give you a short tour of the premises, unless you would like first to refresh yourselves with a cup of tea. I will, of course, provide a sippy cup of fresh milk for *la piccola principessa.*"

Since my little princess wasn't ready to sit still, Bree and I opted for the tour. Francesco provided a running commentary on the hotel's history as he showed us the pub, the spa, the indoor swimming pool, and the magnificent Tudor great hall that served as the hotel's dining room and restaurant. We encountered quite a few guests during our peregrinations, but none of them were accompanied by a hotel employee. Personal concierges, it seemed, came along with the hotel's suites.

By the time we returned to the lobby, I was ready for the cup of tea Francesco had offered. He led us into a spacious, book-lined room.

"Our library," he explained. "Please feel free to borrow a book at any time. If you will be kind enough to leave it in your suite at the end of your stay, we will return it to its proper place on the shelves."

He then excused himself and left us on our own. Bree and I seated ourselves in a pair of leather armchairs near the soot-stained stone hearth and Bess flopped on the hearth rug to examine its intricate pattern.

"There was a time in my life," I mused aloud, "when I lived out of cardboard boxes and slept on a lumpy mattress on the floor."

"There was a time in my life," said Bree, "when I slept on park benches."

I craned my neck to take in the library's leather-bound books and antique furnishings, then settled back in my chair and murmured contentedly, "This is better."

Bree and I exchanged sidelong glances, then grinned like a pair of unrepentant truants. *It's only when you've had nothing,* I thought, *that you truly appreciate having something.*

"You'd think our suite would be ready by now, wouldn't you?" Bree said, leaning forward to peer through the library's doorway to the lobby.

"Eric and Lazlo are probably ironing our blue jeans and scattering rose petals over our sneakers," I said. "I say we take advantage of the delay."

"How?" said Bree.

"Let's have a little chat with Francesco," I said. "Hotel people hear things. Maybe he's heard of Annabelle Trotter."

Francesco returned, accompanied by a middle-aged, uniformed waitress bearing a silver salver laden with a delicate bone china tea service and a pink plastic sippy cup. While the waitress arranged the tea things on a round rosewood table, Francesco bent low to present *la piccola principessa* with the plastic cup and a stuffed animal that would have warmed Mrs. Craven's heart.

"It's a Friesian, isn't it?" I said, pointing to the fluffy black-and-white cow Francesco held out to my daughter.

"It is, madam," he said. "Old Cowerton has long been known for its champion Friesians. Welcome to Old Cowerton, *Principessa,*" he added, smiling down at Bess. "I hope you enjoy your stay at the White Hart."

Bess studied the proffered cow suspiciously, then seized it, bounced it on the hearth rug, and said, quite distinctly, "Moo!"

"Your daughter is a clever girl," said Francesco, straightening.

"I'd like to think so," I said, "but honesty compels me to admit that she says the same thing when she sees a horse."

The waitress left the room, chuckling, and Francesco smiled.

"For your convenience, madam," he said, "the White Hart has a board-certified nanny on call."

"Thank you, but I won't need a nanny," I

told him.

"For backup," Francesco said, and Bree snorted into her teacup. "If it is *la signorina*'s nap time and you wish to visit the shops, press *one* on your mobile and I will send Nanny Sutton to you."

"I'll bear it in mind." I nodded at a nearby armchair. "Please, sit with us."

"Madam is most kind," he said. He lowered himself onto the armchair, but he sat at attention, as if he were ready to spring to his feet at a moment's notice. "How may I assist you?"

"We need your advice," I told him. "An elderly lady who lives in our village grew up here, in Old Cowerton. Her father managed a herd of Friesians for a local landowner. I suppose you could say that we're taking a walk down memory lane on her behalf."

"Most kind," Francesco murmured.

"We'd like to look up some of her old friends," I went on, "but we don't know where they live."

"We don't even know if they're alive," Bree put in. "As Lori said, our friend is elderly."

"You must speak with Mr. Nash," Francesco said promptly. "He is retired now, but for many years he ran the newsagent's shop on the high street. It is still called Nash's

News, after him." Francesco shrugged expressively. "You know how it is with news-agents. They know everything about everyone. If your friend's friends have not left Old Cowerton, Mr. Nash will be able to direct you to them."

"Can you direct us to Mr. Nash?" I asked.

"Nothing could be simpler," Francesco said happily. "It is Sunday, no? Mr. Nash will attend the ten o'clock service at St. Leonard's. At eleven o'clock, he will have brunch at the Willows Café. He will take a table near the front windows." Francesco smiled. "He likes to keep an eye on his old business. After brunch, if the day is sunny, he will sit on the bench near the news-agent's shop."

"Where he can keep a *close* eye on his old business," said Bree.

"Exactly so, madam," said Francesco, nodding.

"And if the day isn't sunny?" Bree inquired.

"He goes home," Francesco replied simply. "Everyone on the high street knows Mr. Nash's routine."

"Where is the Willows Café?" Bree asked.

"I will show you," said Francesco. For a moment I thought he was going to escort us up the high street, but his meaning became clear when he drew a colorful street map from his inside breast pocket. He unfolded the map, laid it flat on the tea table, and traced Mr. Nash's Sunday route with his index finger as he spoke. "The Willows Café is five doors down from the White Hart. The newsagent's is directly across the street from the café." He refolded the map and presented it to Bree, saying, "For you, madam."

Bree thanked him and slipped the map into her day pack.

"It may not be necessary for you to seek out Mr. Nash," Francesco continued. "Perhaps I can help. I have lived in Old Cowerton for many years and I know many people. Not as many as Mr. Nash, to be sure, but quite a few. May I ask your friend's name?"

"Her name has changed a few times over the years," I said, "but she was once known as Annabelle Trotter."

Francesco stiffened.

"Does the name ring a bell?" I asked, watching him closely.

"I have heard it mentioned," he said quietly, looking down at his beautifully manicured hands, "from time to time."

"Have you?" said Bree. "What a surprise. We didn't realize that Annabelle was famous in her hometown. What have you heard about her?"

"I have heard . . . stories," he said haltingly. "I am quite certain none of them are true, madam, but —" He broke off as his cell phone buzzed. He glanced at it, then stood, his practiced smile back in place. "The preparations are complete. Your suite awaits you. Please come with me."

I picked up the sippy cup Bess had discarded and placed it on the tea tray. She clung determinedly to her fluffy cow, however, so I carried her and her new best friend in my arms as Francesco led us across the lobby and down a long, crooked corridor to a door at the rear of the hotel's ground floor.

"Your suite, madam," he said. He bowed us through the doorway and followed us into a small foyer. "Please allow me to show you your home away from home."

Our suite resembled a compact but luxurious cottage. Francesco pointed out the amenities in the kitchenette, the dining nook, the sitting room, and the two bedrooms, each of which had its own private bathroom. A door in the sitting room led to a flagstone patio in the hotel's walled garden, and a door in the garden wall led to the cobbled yard where Eric and Lazlo had parked the Range Rover. Our key cards,

Francesco explained, would open every door.

The baby furniture Bree had requested had been distributed throughout the suite — the changing table, the diaper pail, and the crib in the larger of the two bedrooms; the high chair in the dining nook; and the playpen in the sitting room. Each piece looked — and smelled — as if it had been dunked in antiseptic and scrubbed with cotton swabs. After a few covert sniffs, I decided that the bottle of disinfectant I'd brought with me could remain in the Rover.

A brand-new pink sippy cup had been left on the high chair's tray, Bess's clothes had been stowed in their own special chest of drawers, the contents of her insulated food bag had been transferred to the kitchenette's refrigerator, her all-terrain pram had been parked in the foyer, and her toys had been strewn artfully in the playpen. When she saw her familiar playthings, she began squirming relentlessly to get to them. I put her and her fluffy cow in the hotel's baby jail without a second thought. Our home away from home was clearly cleaner than the home I'd left behind.

Bowls of fresh fruit and vases filled with fresh flowers had been strategically placed in spots that were beyond a toddler's reach.

Although my clothes and Bree's hadn't been strewn with rose petals, they'd been neatly folded in drawers or hung in closets, and our toiletries had been lined up on glass shelves in the bathrooms, beside the swankier products provided by the hotel.

The suite's decor was pleasantly light and airy. Watercolor paintings of pastoral scenes hung between the exposed beams in the white plaster walls, and cream-colored curtains hung at the windows. An antique armoire concealed the television in the sitting room and an elegant escritoire contained a computer workstation. The armchairs and the sofa were upholstered in a pale, rose-patterned chintz fabric that matched the beds' ruffled canopies; thick rugs were scattered across the dark oak floorboards; and a padded fender ensured that Bess wouldn't tumble into the gas-lit fireplace.

At the conclusion of the suite tour, Francesco returned my car keys to me and asked if there was anything else he could do for us.

"You can answer one more question," I said. "Does the Willows Café welcome babies?"

"All of Old Cowerton welcomes babies,

madam." He shrugged. "It is good for business."

"In that case, we're all set." I glanced at my watch. "We'll relax for an hour, then join Mr. Nash for brunch at the Willows Café."

Francesco looked down at his folded hands. When he lifted his head to meet my gaze, he was no longer smiling. "I hope I do not overstep my bounds, madam, but I feel that I must give you a word of warning. Some subjects arouse strong feelings in the town. You may find that Mrs. Trotter is one of them. Outsiders must tread carefully."

With another bow, and a swift smile for Bess, he left the suite.

I watched him go, then turned to look at Bree.

"Well," I said, "we can't say we weren't warned."

" 'Outsiders must tread carefully'?" Bree repeated incredulously. "It's like something out of a spy novel."

"Francesco has obviously heard some dodgy stories about Annabelle," I said.

"Too bad he kept them to himself," said Bree.

"Maybe he's afraid to repeat them," I said. "You know what they say about sleeping dogs. If you wake them, you may get bitten."

Bree folded her arms and eyed me speculatively. "So . . . what do we do next?"

I dropped my shoulder bag on the coffee table and sat in one of the chintz-covered armchairs. "We do exactly what I said we'd do. We let Bess settle into her new surroundings, then we have brunch."

"At the Willows Café?" Bree asked hopefully.

"Where else?" I replied.

"I knew you wouldn't back down!" she crowed.

I smiled grimly as Bree pumped her fist in triumph. Francesco had no doubt meant well, I told myself, but I hadn't come to Old Cowerton to hide out at the White Hart Hotel. I was a Finch-trained snoop. If I had to, I'd wade through a whole kennel of sleeping dogs to awaken the truth about Annabelle Craven's dubious past.

EIGHT

I called Amelia to let her know where we were staying, then tried several times to reach my husband. After listening to a sequence of strange crackling noises followed by fast busy signals, I gave up, tucked my cell phone into my shoulder bag, and vowed to try again later.

We left by the garden door. Had I been on vacation, I would have paused to admire the hotel's display of spring blossoms, and I would have cried out in delight at the sight of the flowering cherry tree, but I couldn't allow myself to stop and smell the hyacinths. I had a job to do, so I put my head down and got on with it.

Bess wasn't thrilled to be confined to her pram, but clean diapers and the companionship of her fluffy Friesian reconciled her to her fate. Impressed by Bess's massive vocabulary, Bree had dubbed the cow "Moo."

It quickly became apparent that Francesco

hadn't been joking when he'd said that all of Old Cowerton welcomed babies. We were stopped several times on the high street by passing strangers, most of whom were old ladies who gazed lovingly at Bess and told me how lucky I was to have such a charming daughter. I would have asked them if they remembered a woman named Annabelle Trotter, but they moved on before Bree or I could start a conversation.

Our stop-and-go stroll down the high street brought us to the Willows Café at twenty minutes past eleven. Mr. Nash's after-church haunt was far more modern than Finch's quaint tearoom. Though located in a lovely old building, the Willows Café was sleek, uncluttered, and brightly lit. It was also seething with holiday makers, most of whom were studying maps or leafing through guidebooks. Even so, we had no trouble spotting the elderly gentleman dining alone at a table near the front windows. We arrived just in time to replace a family that was vacating the table next to his.

A gangly, red-haired young waitress named Megan brought a high chair to our table before we asked for one, and she didn't flinch when I ordered steamed vegetables, mashed parsnips, shredded chicken, and a fruit plate for Bess. Bree and I ordered ham-and-asparagus quiches for ourselves. While Megan filled Bess's pink sippy cup with water, I opened the diaper bag and added an extra-large bib to my daughter's ensemble.

"Messy eater, is she?" Megan asked pleasantly.

"I may have to hose her down later," I replied.

Megan grinned, then bent low to look Bess in the eye. "Good for you, darling. I like a girl who enjoys her food. Your meal will be ready in two ticks," she added and headed for the kitchen.

Neither Bree nor I had to start a conversation with Mr. Nash. Bess started it for us by flinging Moo in his general direction.

"Here you go, little lady," he said as he returned the vagrant cow to its rightful owner. His voice was cracked and quavering, and his face was so deeply wrinkled that his eyes nearly disappeared when he smiled.

"Thank you," I said, putting Moo in the pram. "My daughter would thank you, too, but she appointed me to act as her spokeswoman."

"She's a dear," he said. "She reminds me of my great-granddaughter." He held a liver-spotted hand out to me.

"Bob Nash."

I shook his hand and introduced myself, Bess, and Bree.

"Visitors?" Mr. Nash inquired cordially.

"Yes," I said.

He nodded. "Where are you staying?"

"The White Hart," Bree replied.

"Very nice," he said admiringly. "I've never stayed there myself, but I've heard that the spa is first-rate. Is that why you came to Old Cowerton? Because of the spa at the White Hart?"

"Not exactly." I looked at Bree. "We know an old lady who used to live here."

"She's too old to travel," Bree chimed in, "so we thought we'd take photos of the place where she grew up, to surprise her."

Bree's flight of fancy surprised me, but I tried not to show it.

"Is that so?" Mr. Nash leaned toward us with an interested expression on his face. "As it happens, I've lived in Old Cowerton all my life. It may be that I know this old lady of yours. What's she called?"

"As a young woman," I said, "she was known as Annabelle Trotter."

Mr. Nash's entire aspect changed. He shrank away from us, his wrinkled face flushed a dull red, his nostrils flared, and sparks seemed to fly from his faded blue eyes.

"You know Annabelle, do you?" he asked coldly.

"Yes," I said. "She's a good friend of ours."

"Then you should choose your friends more wisely," he snapped.

"What do you mean?" Bree asked.

"If you knew the truth about Annabelle," he said, "you wouldn't be her friend."

"She seems like a very nice woman to me," I said.

"*Seems,*" he sneered. "Annabelle may *seem* like a nice person, but take it from me: She's rotten to the core."

"I'm sorry, Mr. Nash, but I don't know what you're talking about," Bree said. "Did Annabelle offend you in some way?"

"She did worse than offend me," he growled. "She murdered my best friend!" He glanced at his half-eaten omelet, then stood, flung a ten-pound note on the table, grabbed his jacket from the back of his chair, and stomped out of the café.

"I think we aroused some strong feelings," Bree murmured, looking shell-shocked.

"Here you go," said a voice.

I looked up to see red-haired Megan, who'd returned with our orders. As she transferred dishes from her tray to our table,

I noted with astonished gratitude that Bess's food had been cut into bite-sized pieces and arranged like a necklace around the mound of mashed parsnips.

"I saw you chatting with Mr. Nash just now," Megan went on, sliding the empty tray under her arm and clamping it to her side. "Word to the wise: Mind what you say to him. He's a nice man, but he does love to gossip. If you're not careful, your private business will be the talk of the town. It's what comes of being a newsagent for so many years — an occupational hazard, you might call it. When I first came to Old Cowerton, he —" She broke off as she caught sight of the abandoned omelet. "Oh, dear. Did something upset Mr. Nash? I've never known him to leave without finishing his meal."

"I'm afraid *we* upset him," I confessed.

"What did you do?" Megan asked with an impish grin. "Complain about his old shop?"

"We haven't been to his old shop," Bree said, "so we couldn't complain about it."

I nodded. "He was fine until we happened to mention a woman who lives in our village."

"Then he went ballistic," said Bree.

"Very strange," said Megan, turning to

clear Mr. Nash's table. "Why should a woman who lives in your village put him off his brunch?"

"She lived in Old Cowerton a long time ago," I explained.

"Did she?" said Megan. "What's her name?"

"Annabelle Trotter," I said tentatively, braced for another explosion.

"Never heard of her," said Megan, "but I've only been here since Christmas. I suppose she could be an ex-girlfriend or an ex-wife." She giggled. "Or an ex-mistress. Who knows what he got up to when he was a young man?"

"I'm sure he didn't get up to anything with *our friend*," I said dampingly, hoping to nip a fresh rumor in the bud. "She's not that sort of woman."

"Sorry," said Megan, blushing. "My mouth runs on sometimes."

"Not a problem," I told her. "So does mine."

"Word to the wise," Bree said to the waitress. "Don't let your mouth run on about Annabelle Trotter when Mr. Nash is around."

"Don't worry, I won't," Megan said over her shoulder. "I wouldn't want him to go to the pub for brunch. He's a good customer."

108

"We didn't mean to upset him," I said. "We were just trying to find some of Mrs. Trotter's old friends."

"So we can give her an update on them when we get home," Bree put in.

Megan gave Mr. Nash's table a final wipe with a damp cloth, then turned to face us. "If it's ancient history you're after, you should talk to Hayley Calthorp." She pointed across the street to the newsagent's shop. "Hayley runs Nash's News — the shop Mr. Nash used to own. Her family has lived in Old Cowerton since the year dot. What she doesn't know about the town isn't worth knowing." Megan bent to pick up a chunk of broccoli, a blueberry, and a piece of chicken that had slipped from Bess's grasp and landed on the floor, then urged us to enjoy our meal and bustled away.

"I don't know about you," said Bree when Megan was out of earshot, "but I didn't expect to hear someone confirm Mrs. Craven's crazy story on our first day in town." She leaned toward me and whispered, "Mr. Nash accused Annabelle of *killing his best friend*. He must have meant Zach Trotter."

"If Zach Trotter was his best friend," I said, "he shouldn't be lecturing anyone on choosing friends wisely. Zach Trotter was a drunk, a bully, a liar, and a cheat."

"So says Mrs. Craven," said Bree. "How do we know she's telling the truth?"

"We don't," I acknowledged uncomfortably. "I suppose we should try to find out more about Zach while we're here."

"It seems only fair," said Bree, starting in on her quiche. "I can understand why Francesco warned us to tread carefully. I'll bet Mr. Nash told him about Mrs. Craven's dirty deed."

I removed a streak of mashed parsnip from Bess's hair and started in on my own quiche. I was more disturbed by Mr. Nash's outburst than I cared to admit, but I was also hungry.

"I'll bet Mr. Nash has told everyone in Old Cowerton about Annabelle," I said between bites. "You heard Megan. Mr. Nash loves to gossip."

"He'd feel right at home in Finch," said Bree.

"He certainly would," I said thoughtfully. "Which makes me wonder if we can believe what he said about Annabelle. Gossip can be useful, but it can also cause a lot of trouble. For all we know, Mr. Nash could be a malicious crackpot who makes himself feel important by telling outrageous lies about people."

"Why would he target Mrs. Craven?" Bree asked.

"Who knows?" I said. "Maybe he has a grudge against her. Maybe he was madly in love with her and she rejected him."

"Maybe she criticized his shop," said Bree with a gurgle of laughter. She took another bite of quiche before continuing indistinctly, "But you have to admit that he sounded pretty sure of himself."

"Mr. Barlow was pretty sure of himself when he accused Dick Peacock of stealing his hammer," I reminded her. "But he was mistaken. Dick may have lost track of the hammer for five years, but he didn't steal it."

"Stealing a hammer isn't the same thing as committing a murder," Bree said. "Mr. Nash nearly burst a blood vessel when he heard Annabelle's name. I think he really believes what he told us."

"Bree," I said patiently, "you've lived in Finch long enough to know that people *really believe* all sorts of nonsense."

"True," said Bree. "Look at Megan. She came up with an ex-girlfriend, an ex-wife, and an ex-mistress in about three seconds — and she'd never even heard of Mrs. Craven."

"Exactly." I peered through the window at

111

the shop across the street. "Let's see what Hayley Calthorp has to say before we pass judgment on Annabelle."

NINE

I didn't have to hose Bess down when she finished eating, but it took a while to remove fragments of her meal from her face, neck, ears, hands, and hair. Megan doubled her already ample tip by rinsing the extra-large bib in the kitchen and patting it dry with a paper towel. After thanking her profusely, I popped Bess into the pram and followed Bree out of the Willows Café.

Bess did not want to be in her pram. She wanted to take a postprandial toddle, but traffic was considerably heavier in Old Cowerton than it was in Finch — where it was virtually nonexistent — and I had no intention of crossing the high street in slow motion. While we waited for a break in the stream of passing vehicles, I jutted my chin toward the wooden bench in front of Nash's News.

"Francesco told us that Mr. Nash likes to sit there after brunch," I said. "But look —

no Mr. Nash."

"He's probably going door to door to warn his neighbors about the two mad-women he met at the café," Bree said. "Annabelle Trotter's friends have invaded Old Cowerton! Beware! Beware!"

"Or he may have gone home," I said, tilting my head back to study the sky. "It's getting cloudy. I think an April shower may be heading our way."

"Wish I'd brought an umbrella," said Bree. "The pram has a rain cover, but my head doesn't."

"The perils of packing light," I teased as a driver stopped and waved to us to cross. "Come on. You may be able to buy one at Nash's News."

Bess continued to demand her freedom while we crossed the high street, and when I peered through the newsagent's windows, I realized that it would be a grave mistake to take her into the shop. The shelves lining its cramped aisles were chockablock with temptations a thirteen-month-old would be unable to resist: toys, candies, snacks, postcards, greeting cards, scented candles, souvenirs, and travel-size toiletries as well as newspapers, magazines, and paperback books.

"If I let Bess loose in there," I said, "she'll

114

empty the shelves more quickly than an earthquake."

"No worries," said Bree. "Bess and I will tour the high street while you tackle Hayley Calthorp."

"Are you sure?" I asked.

"Absolutely," said Bree. "Bess needs a walk and I need an umbrella."

"Use mine if you have to," I said. "It's in the diaper bag."

"What will you use?" Bree asked.

"My jacket has a hood," I pointed out. "I'll be okay."

Bree released Bess's harness, set her on her feet, gave her two fingers to hold, and pushed the pram with one hand while my daughter teetered happily by her side. I berated myself silently for teasing my friend, stood aside as a young couple left Nash's News, and let myself into the shop.

A chubby, middle-aged woman with a blond ponytail stood behind the checkout counter to my right. She wore a kelly-green cable-knit sweater and black trousers, and she had very attentive eyes — noticing eyes, as they were called in Finch. Since she was the only person in the shop, apart from myself, I felt safe in assuming that she was Hayley Calthorp.

"Can I help you, dear?" she asked.

"Do you carry umbrellas?" I inquired.

"They're right over there," she said, pointing to a bin filled with colorful compact umbrellas.

"Thank you," I said, selecting a violet brolly for Bree. "I think I'll buy some snacks, too." To get the gossip ball rolling, I used the time-honored technique of dispensing more information than was strictly necessary. "My husband and sons are on a camping trip, so my friend and I brought my daughter with us to enjoy a little holiday of our own. We're staying at the White Hart."

"Get your snacks here," the woman advised. "They'll charge you the earth for them at the White Hart, and you won't find out about it until you get your bill." She motioned toward the shop windows. "Was that your little girl I saw just now?"

"That's my Bess," I acknowledged. I lifted a wire basket from a stack next to the front door and began filling it with assorted munchies. "My friend took her for a walk to keep her from wrecking your shop."

"How old is Bess?" the woman asked.

"Thirteen months," I replied, "give or take a few days."

"I remember when my Lisa was your daughter's age," said the woman. "A perfect terror. Got into everything. I'm sure Bess is lovely, but you can't expect a thirteen-month-old to behave herself in a place like this, can you? You wouldn't believe how many parents bring their children in here, then blame me for the mess they make — a mess that could have been prevented if the parents had a little common sense."

"Common sense isn't as common as it's cracked up to be," I observed.

"It certainly isn't." The woman extended her hand over the counter, saying, "I'm Hayley."

"Lori," I responded, shaking her hand.

Hayley leaned forward with her elbows on the counter, a pose that seemed to suggest a willingness to forgo work for talk. I hooked the basket over my arm and settled in for a cozy chat.

"You're a Yank, aren't you?" she asked.

"My accent always gives me away," I said with a smile. "Yes, I'm a Yank, but my husband and I have lived in England for a long time. We live near a small village not far from here."

"Which village is that, then?" Hayley asked.

"Finch," I replied.

"Sorry," she said, shaking her head. "I've never heard of it."

"Most people haven't," I told her. "It's a very small village."

"There are lots of them about," she said. "What do you and your friend plan to do while you're here? Treat yourselves to facials at the spa?"

"No," I said. "We came to Old Cowerton to do a favor for a friend who lives in our village." Taking a page out of Bree's book, I continued, "Our friend used to live here. She's too old to travel, so we thought we'd surprise her by taking photographs of people and places she knew way back when. Megan at the Willows Café said that you might be able to point us in the right direction."

"Megan's a great girl," said Hayley.

"She's terrific," I agreed, "but the strangest thing happened to us at the café. We sat next to a man named Bob Nash and we got to talking with him —"

"There's no other choice with Bob," Hayley interrupted, rolling her eyes. "The man could talk the hind leg off a hippo."

"He was very friendly," I went on, "until we told him about our elderly friend. Her name is Annabelle —"

"Not Annabelle Craven!" Hayley exclaimed.

To my relief, she seemed pleased rather

than incensed.

"Yes," I said. "Annabelle Craven is our neighbor. Do you know her?"

"She grew up not ten doors down from my gran," said Hayley, smiling delightedly. "She and my gran went to school together. They were great friends."

"I'd love to meet one of Annabelle's old school friends," I said, feeling as though I'd hit the mother lode. "Would your gran mind if I took a picture of her?"

"You're too late, I'm afraid," said Hayley, her smile dimming. "Gran passed away nearly fifteen years ago."

"I'm so sorry," I said.

"She had a good life," Hayley assured me, "and she passed peacefully." She released a soft sigh, then brightened. "I can't believe that you know Annabelle Craven. She must be getting on in years. How is she?"

"She's very well," I said.

"I'm glad to hear it," said Hayley. "Please tell her that Hayley Calthorp sends her love. I can't tell you how much we miss her here in Old Cowerton."

"Mr. Nash doesn't seem to miss her," I said.

"He wouldn't," Hayley said, with a disparaging tut. "He believes in the widow's curse."

"I beg your pardon?" I said, mystified.

Before Hayley Calthorp could demystify me, the front door opened and a half dozen boisterous boys spilled into the shop. They were closer in age to Will and Rob than to Bess, and Hayley knew each of them by name, so they posed no threat to her jam-packed shelves, but they were so noisy I could scarcely hear myself think. I had to wait for them to make their purchases — chocolate bars and comic books — and leave before I could resume my conversation with Hayley.

"I'm not sure I know what you mean by 'the widow's curse,' " I said.

"Why should you?" she asked. "It's a load of old rubbish."

"If it's a load of old rubbish," I said, "why does Mr. Nash believe in it?"

"Because he's a superstitious old duffer," Hayley stated firmly. She leaned on the counter and continued, "According to my gran, the whole thing started toward the end of the Second World War, when a local chap named Zach Trotter came home on leave from training camp. He took Anna-belle to a dance and the next thing Gran knew, they were married. It was one of those rushed wartime marriages. Annabelle's parents didn't approve — Annabelle was barely seventeen — but you know what young people are like."

"They don't often listen to their parents," I commented, "especially when they're in love."

"Gran didn't think much of wartime marriages," Hayley went on. " 'Marry in haste, repent at leisure' is what she always said, and that's exactly what happened to Annabelle. Zach was a nice enough boy when he joined up — big, tall, good-looking, polite — but the war changed him, and not for the better."

"I imagine he wasn't the only soldier who had trouble adjusting to civilian life after the war," I commented.

"Zach had more trouble than most," Hayley said darkly.

"What sort of trouble?" I asked.

"All sorts," she replied. "After everything he'd been through, normal life must have been too tame for him. He started drinking, gambling, fighting. People got used to seeing him stagger home from the pub after closing time."

"Where was home?" I asked. "I mean, where did he and Annabelle live?"

"They lived with her parents for a while, because of the housing shortage," Hayley informed me. "But Zach was a veteran, so he got first crack at one of the houses built after the war. Homes for heroes, they were called, but they were just poky little row houses thrown up in a boggy field. A local landowner donated the land. Gran said he couldn't wait to get rid of it."

I recalled the small enclave of row houses Bree and I had passed on our way to Old Cowerton. "I think I saw the homes for heroes when we drove into town."

"Did you drive in from the Oxford road?" Hayley inquired. When I nodded, she said, "You passed right by them. We call them the terraces nowadays. Hardly anyone remembers that they were homes for heroes."

"Why are the terraces off on their own?" I asked. "Why is there a gap between them and the rest of Old Cowerton?"

"The town hated them," Hayley replied. "The way Gran put it was 'We were willing to build cheap housing as long as we didn't have to look at it.' " She chuckled reminiscently, then went on. "The terraces have been improved over the years with insulation and indoor toilets and such, but back then, they weren't very nice."

"Do you know which house Annabelle lived in?" I asked, thinking of the map Francesco had presented to Bree. "I'd like to take a picture of it."

"It's easy enough to find," Hayley informed me. "There aren't but three streets in the terraces — four if you count Longview Lane. You'll find Annabelle's house at the west end of Bellevue Terrace. That's the end closest to town," she added helpfully.

"Thanks," I said. "It'll mean a lot to Annabelle to see what the place looks like now."

"She called her house Dovecote," Hayley continued. "She made a sign and hung it above the house number, Gran said, to give her house a loving touch. Poor Annabelle." Hayley shook her head sadly. "She must have thought that she and Zach would get on like a pair of turtledoves, but it didn't work out that way."

"What happened?" I asked.

The front door opened again and an elderly couple came into the shop, seeking a particular brand of shampoo. Hayley found it for them and rang it up, then scurried over to open the door for them before returning to her post behind the counter.

"Where was I?" she asked.

"Annabelle and Zach moved into Dovecote on Bellevue Terrace in the terraces," I said.

"That's right," said Hayley, leaning on the counter. "Zach worked odd jobs, but Gran said he drank most of his earnings. Annabelle had to support them with her needlework. Have you seen her needlework?"

"I have three of her baby quilts," I said.

"I have two," said Hayley, her face glowing. "They're beautiful, aren't they?"

"I framed mine," I told her.

Hayley nodded her approval, then continued, "Annabelle didn't have time for quilting back then. She worked her fingers to the bone making and mending, just to put food on the table. Then one day, about a year after they married, Zach ups and leaves." She snapped her fingers. "Just like that."

"He ran out on her?" I said, as if I hadn't already heard Mrs. Craven's version of the story.

"Just like that," Hayley repeated, snapping her fingers again. "Gran said it was exactly the sort of thing a feckless layabout like Zach Trotter would do."

"It must have been hard on Annabelle," I said.

"Gran said it was the best thing that ever happened to her," Hayley declared, "and it might have been, if Minnie Jessop hadn't opened her big mouth and started yapping."

My ears pricked up at the sound of an unfamiliar name. Minnie Jessop had played no role in the tale Mrs. Craven had told me at the quilting bee.

"Who is Minnie Jessop?" I asked.

"Minnie lived next door to the Trotters," Hayley explained. She wrinkled her nose, as if a foul odor had wafted into the shop. "You wouldn't want to live next door to Minnie Jessop. Gran used to call her the town crier. Eyes on stalks, ears like radar dishes, and a mind like a sewer. After Zach disappeared, Minnie got it into her thick skull that Annabelle had done away with him."

"You're kidding," I said in appropriately shocked tones.

"I wish I were," said Hayley. "According to Gran, Minnie caused all sorts of strife for poor Annabelle. You know how it is with rumors."

"Once they start," I said, "they're hard to stop."

"And the uglier they are, the more willing people are to believe them," Hayley said feelingly. "Once Minnie Jessop cried murder, word got around. And once word got around, the police had to look into it. They found nothing, of course, because there was nothing to find. Zach may have been a useless lump, but Annabelle couldn't have killed him. She didn't have it in her to kill anyone."

"Did the rumors die down after the police cleared her?" I asked.

"They should have, but Minnie Jessop and her cronies kept them going," said Hayley. "Annabelle was too proud to go back to her parents' place and she couldn't afford to live anywhere else, so she kept her head down and ignored the wagging tongues as best she could. Then Ted Fletcher came along."

"Ted Fletcher?" I said alertly. "Who is Ted Fletcher?"

"Ted Fletcher was Bob Nash's best friend," said Hayley. "The two of them were like brothers. They'd grown up together, gone to school together, gone to war together. There was some talk of Ted marrying Bob's sister Gladys, but it came to nothing."

"Because of Annabelle?" I asked.

"That's right," said Hayley. "There may have been an understanding between Ted Fletcher and Gladys Nash before he joined up, but it ended when Ted fell for Annabelle."

"Annabelle was still married to Zach Trotter, wasn't she?" I asked.

"She was, in the eyes of the law," Hayley

confirmed. "She couldn't divorce Zach because no one knew where he was, and she couldn't ask a court to declare him dead until he'd been missing for seven years." Hayley leaned closer to me, saying earnestly, "There was no funny business between her and Ted Fletcher. He went to church with Annabelle, took her to the cinema, fixed things around the house when they needed fixing — but he never stayed overnight. Ted was a good and decent man. He was willing to wait for Annabelle. Gran reckoned they would have married if he hadn't died."

"He *died*?" I said in authentically shocked tones. "How?"

"Ted worked as a cowman up at the dairy," said Hayley. "About a year after he met Annabelle, he fell into a slurry pit and drowned."

"A slurry pit?" I repeated uncomprehendingly. "I'm sorry, but I don't know what a slurry pit is."

"It's like a pond," she explained, "only it's full of cow manure."

I recoiled, torn between pity and revulsion at the thought of a man drowning in a pool of cow dung.

"Good heavens," I said faintly. "What a dreadful way to die."

Hayley raised her shoulders in a fatalistic

shrug. "Dairy farms can be dangerous places. Accidents happen. But because he was Annabelle's sweetheart, people started asking themselves if Ted Fletcher's death *was* an accident."

A middle-aged woman in a rain-speckled blue anorak came into the shop with a long list of travel toiletries. I'd been too absorbed in Hayley Calthorp's riveting tale to pay attention to the weather, but when I saw the woman's anorak, I realized that the April shower had arrived. While Hayley helped her customer, I backed into a corner, pulled my cell phone out of my shoulder bag, and called Bree.

"Bess and I are at the hotel," she informed me. "We bailed when it began to rain."

"Good decision," I said.

"Francesco brought us warm milk and a pot of tea," she went on, "and I lit a fire in the hearth, so we're snug as two bugs. How's it going at Nash's News?"

"Informatively," I told her. "I'll fill you in when I get back."

"Remember to put your hood up," Bree advised.

She rang off before I could tell her that I had a new umbrella. I dropped my phone into my shoulder bag and waited impatiently for the woman in the damp anorak to depart, then returned to the counter, agog to hear more about Ted Fletcher's ghastly death.

Hayley had evidently lost her train of thought again, so I helped her to find it.

"Ted Fletcher's accident," I prompted.

"That's right," she said, planting her elbows on the counter. "It happened only a few months after he and Annabelle started seeing each other. Minnie Jessop couldn't wait to say 'I told you so' to everyone who doubted her when she accused Annabelle of killing Zach. She put it about that any man who took an interest in Annabelle would die before his time. She began calling it the widow's curse."

"That's absurd," I objected. "Setting aside the fact that curses only work in fairy tales, Minnie's rumor doesn't add up. Why would Annabelle kill a decent, hardworking man who adored her?"

"Exactly!" Hayley exclaimed. "She wouldn't, of course, but you'd be surprised at how many people believed Minnie and her chums. If you repeat a lie often enough, it starts to look an awful lot like the truth."

"Bob Nash still believes it," I said.

"Ted's death hit Bob hard," said Hayley. "Gran said he needed to blame someone, so he blamed Annabelle for bringing the widow's curse down on his best friend. Gran tried to talk some sense into him, but he listened to Minnie Jessop's ravings instead. Pillock," she muttered disdainfully.

"Is Minnie Jessop still around?" I asked.

"She's still in the same house," said Hayley, "the one next door to Dovecote." She laughed. "They'll need an oyster knife to pry her out of there. Minnie's husband passed away years ago and she must be pushing ninety, but her daughter Susan looks after her, the one that never married."

A flurry of raindrops pelted the shop windows, and several families rushed through the front door, presumably to get in out of the rain. They didn't appear to be in a hurry to leave and I didn't care to have them eavesdrop on my conversation with Hayley, so I paid for the snacks and the umbrella and prepared to venture forth into the storm.

"I'm lucky that Megan sent me to you," I said to Hayley. "You've been incredibly generous with your time. If the sun co-operates tomorrow, my friend and I should get some great photographs of Dovecote. It's at the end of Bellevue Terrace, right?"

"That's right," she said cheerfully. "Look for the rosebushes in the back garden. You'll know them when you see them. They're the healthiest rosebushes in Old Cowerton."

A ripple of uncertainty passed through me as I remembered Mrs. Craven's chilling words: *I thought a dead body would enrich the soil* . . . I mumbled a distracted thank-you to Hayley, threaded my way through the overcrowded shop, pulled my hood up, and stepped outside without opening the violet umbrella. I'd forgotten all about it.

I could think of nothing but the corpse that might lie buried beneath the healthiest rosebushes in Old Cowerton, and the man who died an unspeakable death in a slurry pit.

TEN

The April shower had become a minor gale. By the time I reached the White Hart, my jacket was streaming with rain, my trouser legs were drenched, and my shoes squelched like soaked sponges. To avoid leaving a trail of puddles in the crooked corridor, I entered our suite via the garden door.

The peaceful scene that greeted me helped to ease the turmoil in my brain. A fire burned steadily in the gas-lit hearth. A dainty, antique tea service sat on the teak table in the dining nook. Moo gazed serenely at me from the playpen.

Bree was lying on the sofa, reading a handsome leather-bound edition of *Wuthering Heights*.

"*Wuthering Heights?*" I said, raising an eyebrow.

"Perfect weather for it," she said, pointing a stockinged foot at the rain-washed windows. "I borrowed it from the hotel's library.

I started reading it to Bess, but she dozed off before I finished the first page, so I moved her to the cot in your room and carried on without her." She laid the book aside and stood. "I'll try Jane Austen next. I don't think Bess is a Brontë fan."

"Maybe not," I said, "but she's a big fan of afternoon naps. Thanks for taking such good care of her — and for introducing her to a classic."

"Maybe she'll grow into it," said Bree.

I dropped my dripping shoulder bag on the coffee table and passed the sopping shopping bag to Bree, saying, "Almonds, cashews, raisins, banana chips, a variety of chocolate bars — which must never cross Bess's lips — and a violet umbrella to match your clogs. Would you mind ordering a fresh pot of tea while I change? I feel as if I just crawled through a car wash."

As I squelched into the larger bedroom, I made a mental note to buy a copy of *Wuthering Heights* for the nursery at home. Bess rarely had a restless night, but when she did, a literary sleep aid might come in handy.

She was the exact opposite of restless as she napped in the hotel's crib. I paused to smile down at her, then hung my jacket on the showerhead in the bathroom, draped my wet clothes on the towel warmer, dressed in soft jeans, wool socks, and a fleece pullover, and returned to the sitting room, taking care to shut the bedroom door behind me.

Bree was in the kitchenette, pouring boiling water from an electric kettle into the dainty teapot.

"No need to order a fresh pot," she said over her shoulder. "I found tea bags in the cupboard, and I've barely touched the cream and sugar Francesco delivered earlier." She put the lid on the teapot, then turned to face me. "Well? What's the verdict? Is Mrs. Craven guilty or not guilty?"

"I hate to say it," I said, "but the jury's still out."

"What does Hayley Calthorp think?" Bree asked.

"Hayley Calthorp thinks Mrs. Craven is as pure as the driven snow." I poured myself a cup of weak but steaming tea and carried it into the sitting room. "But Minnie Jessop and her cronies think differently — *very* differently."

"Who's Minnie Jessop?" Bree asked, resuming her perch on the sofa.

I sank into an armchair, wrapped my chilled hands around my teacup, and began, "Minnie Jessop is a purveyor of nasty rumors. . . ." It took me less than twenty minutes to summarize everything I'd learned at Nash's News.

"Poor Ted Fletcher," Bree said when I fell silent. "I don't mean to speak ill of the dead, but . . . *ick.*" She folded her arms across her chest and shuddered. "Can you imagine what it must have been like to pull his body out of the slurry pit?"

"I'd rather not, thanks." I sipped my tea and let my gaze drift toward Moo. "I'll never look at Mr. Malvern's dairy farm in quite the same way again."

"I suppose they have to put the muck somewhere," Bree said. "As for the widow's curse . . ." She tossed her head derisively. "We've gone from a spy novel to a fairy tale — an extra-grim fairy tale."

"The same thought crossed my mind," I said. "I was ready to write off Bob Nash and Minnie Jessop as a pair of cranks until —"

"Until Hayley Calthorp mentioned the rosebushes," Bree broke in, nodding. "That part gave me the creeps, too."

"Psychopaths are supposed to be good at fooling people," I said, staring pensively into the fire. "Mrs. Craven told me that she fooled the nice young constable who questioned her after Zach Trotter disappeared.

She practically bragged about it." I turned my head to look at Bree. "What if she fooled Hayley's gran as well? What if Minnie Jessop is right about Mrs. Craven, and Hayley Calthorp is wrong?"

"No two ways about it," Bree said decisively. "We have to pay a call on Minnie Jessop."

"I agree," I said. "We'll take a look at Dovecote tomorrow morning, then knock on Minnie's door. Something tells me that she won't be reluctant to speak with us."

"She'll probably talk our ears off." Bree ran a hand through her pixie cut and glanced toward the windows. "Are we done for the day, then?"

"I am," I said. "I need to recharge my batteries before I face Old Cowerton again."

Bree bounced to her feet. "While you recharge," she said, "I'll go for a swim."

"Did you bring a bathing suit?" I asked, surprised.

"No," she replied blithely. "I thought I'd liven up the place by skinny dipping. It's a Kiwi thing. We always swim *au naturel.*" She kept a straight face for a heartbeat, then dissolved into giggles. "Of course I brought a swimsuit, Lori! Didn't you?"

"No," I said. "I was too busy packing diapers and whole-grain crackers to think about packing a swimsuit."

"Never mind," Bree said, heading for her bedroom. "If you ask nicely, I'm sure Francesco will fly a seamstress in from Milan to make one for you."

I was dying to see if Bree would don a bikini or a tank suit or a glittering King Neptune costume, but I didn't get the chance. She left the suite swaddled in a White Hart bathrobe.

I finished my tea in one quick gulp, then placed my cup on the coffee table and pulled the blue journal from my shoulder bag. With Bess in dreamland and Bree in the pool, I could tell Aunt Dimity where my incurable curiosity had taken me.

"Dimity?" I said as I opened the journal. "Bree Pym, Bess, and I are sharing a suite at the extremely fancy White Hart Hotel in Old Cowerton — Mrs. Craven's old hometown."

I felt myself relax as Aunt Dimity's familiar copperplate began to scroll across the blank page.

I won't pretend to be surprised, my dear. I knew that your sense of justice wouldn't allow you to sit at home, twiddling your thumbs, while a potential wolf in sheep's clothing lurked among your unsuspecting neighbors. Did you recruit Bree to travel with you? What a clever thing to do!

"I didn't have to recruit Bree," I explained, pleased to be praised for my sense of justice instead of my nosiness. "Once I told her about Mrs. Craven's crazy confession, she insisted on coming with me."

Again, I'm not surprised. Bree is a darling girl and an asset to any investigation. Have you been in Old Cowerton long enough to learn anything of value?

"We've learned quite a few things," I said. "Whether they're of value or not remains to be seen. Our personal concierge —" I broke off as a single line of graceful script raced across the page.

You have a personal concierge?

"We do," I said, blushing. "I told you: The White Hart is extremely fancy."

It must be.

"Our personal concierge is named Francesco," I continued stoically. "When we asked Francesco about Annabelle Trotter, he hinted that we should rethink our plan to ask the townspeople about her. He warned us that her name might arouse strong feelings in Old Cowerton. And he was right."

I described our disturbing encounter with Bob Nash at the Willows Café and recounted my lengthy chat with Hayley Cal-

138

thorp at Nash's News. When I finished, I sat back to await Aunt Dimity's response. Her first comment was somewhat unexpected.

I knew that Bess's presence would help rather than hinder your inquiry. She broke the ice with both Mr. Nash and Hayley Calthorp.

"Bess threw Moo at Mr. Nash," I agreed, "but she didn't even throw a glance at Hayley Calthorp."

Precisely. Hayley decided that you must be a sensible person as well as a responsible parent because you didn't allow Bess to rampage through her shop. Respect and gratitude made her warm to you and loosened her tongue.

"I'll thank Bess when she wakes up," I said, smiling, "but I'm pretty sure that Hayley's tongue would have been loosened by anyone who said nice things about Mrs. Craven."

Your microscopic survey seems to indicate that the town is divided into two factions.

"Two warring factions," I said, remembering Mr. Nash's flushed face. "The Hayley Calthorp faction believes that Annabelle couldn't hurt a fly and that the widow's curse is a load of old rubbish. The Minnie Jessop faction is convinced that she's responsible for bumping off Zach Trotter and cursing Ted Fletcher." I wrinkled my nose. "Poor Ted. Can you think of a worse way to die?"

We can only hope that the fumes rendered him unconscious before he drowned.

"Fumes?" I echoed, aghast.

Slurry pits can emit poisonous gases.

"Good grief," I murmured, pressing a hand to my lips.

Hayley Calthorp wasn't being melodramatic when she said that dairy farms can be dangerous places, Lori. They were even more dangerous in Ted Fletcher's time. There were minimal safety regulations in those days. Slurry pits weren't required to have fences with locked gates, and dairymen were allowed to work alone near them. If a dairyman was overcome by fumes, or if he slipped and fell into a pit, there was no one to sound the alarm, much less to rescue him. People who complain about health and safety laws don't remember — or don't realize — what workplaces were like before *health and safety laws. Elementary precautions were ignored and the workingman paid the price.*

"Ted Fletcher paid the ultimate price," I said, "but it wasn't because of the widow's curse."

Of course it wasn't. Minnie Jessop must have a vivid and a rather morbid imagination.

"I'll let you know," I said. "Bree and I intend to visit her tomorrow morning, after we check out Dovecote." I smiled wryly. "I may have to handcuff Bree to the pram to keep her from climbing into the back garden to dig up the rosebushes."

Her enthusiasm does her credit. I would, however, discourage her from purchasing a spade. To review: Dovecote was the Trotters' home and the Trotters lived next door to Minnie Jessop.

"They lived adjacent to her," I clarified, "in a row house — one of the 'homes for heroes' built on the edge of town after the war."

As I recall, the so-called homes for heroes were produced cheaply and quickly. Most had rudimentary plumbing and paper-thin walls. A row house with paper-thin walls isn't an ideal home for a newlywed couple, but it would be a gift to a dedicated gossip.

"One can't avoid hearing one's neighbors through paper-thin walls," I said, nodding.

I advise you to ask Minnie Jessop what she heard on the night Zach Trotter disappeared.

"We may not have to ask," I said. "Zach Trotter's disappearance seems to be Minnie's favorite subject."

Indeed it does, which is why you must examine Dovecote and its surroundings care-

141

*fully. How many houses overlook the Trotters'
back garden? Did someone other than Minnie
Jessop witness suspicious activity near the
rosebushes on the night in question?*

"Annabelle left Dovecote a long time
ago," I pointed out. "I imagine most of her
former neighbors have either passed away
or moved away."

*You never know. There may be a few neigh-
bors who've hung on, as Minnie Jessop has.*

"If they're alive, Bree and I will do our
best to find them," I promised.

*After you survey Dovecote, you must per-
suade Minnie Jessop to invite you into her
home.*

"Why?" I asked.

*Row houses tend to have identical floor
plans, Lori. Once you're inside Minnie Jessop's house, you'll be able to study a reasonable facsimile of the alleged crime scene.*

"According to Hayley, the houses have
been improved since they were built," I said.
"They may have been remodeled."

*Even so, you should be able to glean rele-
vant information from Minnie Jessop's floor
plan. Hayley Calthorp told you that Zach Trotter was big and tall, didn't she?*

"Yes," I said. "She described prewar Zach
as big, tall, good-looking, and polite."

Let's focus on his size for the moment, shall

we? When you're in Minnie Jessop's house, try to gauge how far the bottom of the staircase is from the back door. Ask yourself if a petite young woman could drag a big, tall, and no doubt heavy corpse such a distance. Look for obstacles that might have impeded her progress. Is there a raised threshold, perhaps, or an impossibly awkward turn?

"I'll give it a test run," I agreed. "I'll try to push the pram through Minnie's house to her back garden."

An excellent notion. If the pram gets stuck, chances are that a corpse would get stuck, too.

"A corpse would be more flexible than a pram, though," I said reflectively. "After the rigor passed off, it would bend around corners."

Oh, dear. What a distressing image.

"We're investigating a possible homicide," I reminded her. "Distressing images come with the territory. Annabelle didn't wrap Zach in tissue paper and slap a bow on his nose after she smashed his head in. She claims that she rolled him onto a rug. All I'm saying is, a body on a rug would bend more easily than Bess's pram."

Forgive me, Lori. You're quite right. It's no time to be squeamish. Perhaps Bree would volunteer to be rolled onto a rug. I'm sure

Minnie Jessop would approve of the reenact-ment.

"She probably would," I said, "but I'm not going to dump Bree on a rug and drag her through a stranger's house, just to prove that it could be done. Besides, Bree isn't big or tall. She's as short as I am and much slimmer."

You must do as you think best, my dear. The pram may produce limited results, but limited results are better than no results at all.

I heard the click of a lock in the foyer and grabbed my shoulder bag.

"Bree's back," I whispered. "Gotta go. More tomorrow."

Before I closed the blue journal, I caught of glimpse of Aunt Dimity's parting words.

Good luck!

I thrust the journal into my shoulder bag and threw the bag onto the coffee table mere seconds before Bree came through from the foyer.

"The pool's heated," she said, flopping limply on the sofa. "I had it all to myself until every mummy and daddy in the known universe decided that swimming would be an excellent rainy-day activity for the kiddies. I was suddenly surrounded by a thousand screaming children doing cannonballs."

"What did you do?" I asked, laughing. "Hide in the sauna?"

"Nope," she replied. "I had a massage. Ask for Mariana. Her hands should be immortalized in marble. What are we doing for dinner?"

"Would you mind room service?" I asked. "Bess has had to deal with a lot of new sights and sounds today. She'll sleep better tonight if we keep her in more or less familiar surroundings."

"Room service works for me," said Bree.

"Will an early night work as well?" I said. "I can just about guarantee that Bess will be up by seven tomorrow."

"I was counting on an early night," said Bree, rubbing her eyes. "If I were Bess's age — or Mrs. Craven's — I'd take a nap right now." She yawned loudly. "I blame Mariana. I'm so unwound I can hardly sit up straight."

"Go ahead," I told her. "You're on holiday. You can take as many naps as you like."

"What will you do while Bess and I are snoozing?" Bree asked, standing.

"Contemplate tomorrow," I said. "And make another attempt to reach Bill."

"Too energetic for me," she said. "See you in forty winks!"

She retreated to her bedroom and I took

my cell phone from my shoulder bag. When Bill proved to be unreachable yet again, I rested my head against the back of the armchair and rehearsed the questions I would ask Minnie Jessop, if she opened her door to us. The sound of rain falling in the walled garden made it difficult to concentrate, however, and the flickering fire was more soothing than a Mariana massage.

Before I knew it, I was napping, too.

ELEVEN

We rose from our naps with energy to spare. A brisk wind had chased the rain away, but it was blowing too hard for comfort, so we stayed indoors. To keep Bess from going stir crazy, Bree and I took her for a long walk up and down the hotel's corridors. We were in the library, searching for a copy of *Pride and Prejudice,* when my cell phone rang. I pulled it out of my trouser pocket and scanned the small screen.

"It's Bill!" I exclaimed.

"Let's hope you can hear him this time," said Bree.

As we were the library's only patrons, I didn't hesitate to fling myself into a chair and answer the call. To my relief, my husband's voice came through loud and clear.

"Lori?" he said. "Sorry about being out of touch. Our campsite was in a dead spot."

"Was?" I queried. "Have you moved to a different campsite?"

"I found a better site in Grasmere," he replied. "It's not quite so far off the beaten track."

"I tried calling you several times at your old campsite," I told him. "Did any of my messages get through to you?"

"Something about a girls' getaway?" he hazarded.

"Bingo," I said. "Bree Pym, Bess, and I are staying at a spa hotel in a place called Old Cowerton. It's not far from Finch."

"Sounds ideal," said Bill.

"How's camping?" I asked.

"It's great," he replied. "We took the ferry across Lake Windermere to join a guided hike with a park ranger on Friday, we went fishing yesterday, and we're going to Ravenglass tomorrow to ride the steam train."

"Will and Rob will love the train," I said. "Let me speak with them, will you?"

"Can't," said Bill. "They're down at the lake, skipping stones. Don't worry," he added hastily, "I can see them, and they're still high and dry. Well, they're *mostly* dry. Is Bess with you?"

"Of course," I said. "I'll put her on."

I held the phone to Bess's ear and watched with pleasure as her face lit up. She told her daddy all about Francesco, Moo, and our run-in with Mr. Nash, but since Bill wasn't

148

as fluent in baby talk as I was, he didn't understand her. He understood me, however, and while I refrained from telling him the real reason for our visit to Old Cowerton, I also refrained from telling him any outright lies.

"They're having a complete blast," I reported to Bree after Bill and I had said our good-byes. "Hiking, fishing, steam trains —"

"No murders, curses, or grisly accidents?" Bree interrupted. "How dull."

"I'm just happy they're having better luck with the weather than we are," I said. "When I think of them sleeping in a tent, I almost feel guilty about our fabulous suite." I stashed the phone in my pocket and grinned. "Almost."

Bess made an unsteady dash for freedom, but Francesco appeared in the nick of time to prevent her escape. As he entered the library, he scooped her up, turned her around, planted her on her feet, and herded her toward me like an affectionate sheepdog.

"Thanks, Francesco," I said, directing Bess's steps away from the doorway. "I'm pretty sure she could find her way back to our suite on her own by now, but I'd rather not risk it."

A dark-haired young man appeared at

Francesco's elbow, carrying a watering can. He hesitated when he saw Bree and me, but a nod from Francesco freed him to make his way around the library, watering the potted plants that added a homey touch to the book-lined room. Bess had a fine time chasing after him.

"Your suite is satisfactory, madam?" Francesco inquired, turning his attention to me. "You have everything you need?"

"We have more than we need," I assured him.

"The weather is not what I would wish for you," he said dolefully.

"The rain made our suite seem even cozier," I said, hoping to cheer him up.

"We don't expect you to control the weather," Bree chimed in. "You're good, Francesco, but no one's *that* good."

He smiled appreciatively, but I detected a note of apprehension in his voice when he asked, "Did you enjoy your brunch at the Willows Café?"

"Brunch was lovely," I said, "but Mr. Nash wasn't very helpful."

"Our waitress was, though," said Bree. "She sent us across the street to speak with Hayley Calthorp."

"Hayley was brilliant," I said. "She filled me in on Zach Trotter's disappearance."

"And the widow's curse that struck down poor Ted Fletcher," Bree interjected.

"She also told us where our friend Annabelle lived when she was married to Zach Trotter," I continued.

"We're going to the terraces tomorrow morning," Bree said brightly. "We hope to have a chat with Minnie Jessop."

"Mrs. Jessop will have much to say," Francesco observed with a mournful sigh. "She will no doubt tell you about the others."

Bree and I exchanged puzzled glances.

"The others?" I said. "What others?"

"I . . . I made a slip of the tongue, madam," Francesco stammered, blushing. "I beg you to ignore it." He snapped his fingers and the silent young man with the watering can left the room. "If I can be of assistance . . ." His voice trailed off as he turned on his heel and fled.

"What's up with him?" Bree asked, looking bewildered. "Who are 'the others'?"

"Not a clue and no idea," I replied. "I'll add 'Who are the others?' to my list of questions for Minnie Jessop."

Bree had found *Pride and Prejudice* and Bess had run out of steam, so we headed back to the suite to order dinner. Lazlo showed up almost instantly to set the table in the dining nook and Eric followed him a short time later with a sumptuous repast. I felt like the Queen of the May until Bess brought me back down to earth with a remarkably well aimed blob of mashed potatoes.

I kept to Bess's normal routine of dinnertime, bath time, story time, bedtime. Less than a paragraph of *Wuthering Heights* put her out like a light. I moved Moo from the crib to the dresser, then joined Bree, who was seated on the sofa, studying Francesco's map of Old Cowerton.

"We shouldn't have much trouble finding our way around the terraces," she announced. "There are only three rows of row houses. They're set one behind the other, like dominoes."

"Show me," I said, sitting beside her.

"Longview Lane acts as an access road," she explained. She drew a fingertip across the pertinent section of the map as she continued, "Bellevue Terrace, Parkview Terrace, and Greenview Terrace feed into Longview Lane, and Longview Lane leads to the main road." Her finger came to rest on the last house in the last row of row houses. "There's Dovecote."

"I wonder who lives there now?" I mused aloud. "I wonder if they're aware of Dovecote's creepy past?"

"With Minnie Jessop living next door?" said Bree, her eyebrows rising. "How could they *not* know?"

One thing was certain, I thought, scanning the pastureland beyond Dovecote. We wouldn't have to scour the terraces to find someone to corroborate or to dispute Minnie's version of events, as Aunt Dimity had advised. The map made it clear that no one other than Minnie Jessop could have witnessed suspicious activity in the Trotters' back garden because hers was the only house that overlooked it.

"The turnoff is just over a mile from the hotel," Bree was saying. "We could walk there easily."

"We could," I allowed, "but I'd rather drive."

"Why?" she asked.

"The terraces are solidly residential," I replied. "There aren't any businesses. If the weather turns ugly again — which it probably will — we won't be able to duck into a shop or a café."

"Got it," Bree said. "If all else fails, we can duck into the Rover."

"*Or,*" I said, drawing the word out for emphasis, "we can try very hard to duck into Minnie Jessop's house." I repeated Aunt Dimity's comments about row houses as if they were my own. I didn't have to explain why it would be useful to see an interior similar to Dovecote's. Bree caught on right away.

"We'll break into Minnie's house, if we have to," she declared as she refolded the map and stuffed it into her day pack. "We can't pass up a chance to see a duplicate scene of the possible crime-next-door."

Plans made, we called it a night. I thought my sleep would be disrupted by nightmares about slurry pits, rosebushes, and Francesco's mysterious "others," but *Wuthering Heights* did the trick for me, too. I slept without stirring until Bess woke me in the morning.

The storm left nothing but clear skies and muddy puddles in its wake. The wind was calm, the air was deliciously warm, and the dew-bedecked flowers in the walled garden sparkled like jewels in the morning sun.

After an early room-service breakfast, followed by a midmorning snack for Bess, we were ready to go. I loaded Moo, the food bag, the diaper bag, and my freshly diapered daughter into the all-terrain pram and followed Bree through the garden to the cobbled yard where Eric and Lazlo had left the Range Rover. While Bree swung Bess into her car seat, I folded the pram and slid it into the cargo compartment.

I didn't mention the role the pram might play in our investigation because I was afraid of putting ideas into Bree's head. If Aunt Dimity could imagine me dragging my young friend through Minnie Jessop's house on a rug, so could Bree. Bree was game enough to *demand* that I use her as a crash-test dummy, but I had no intention of staging such a grotesque reenactment. To avoid an argument, I kept Aunt Dimity's suggestion to myself.

I wanted to shout for joy after I drove the Rover through the narrow alleyway without losing a wing mirror, but I maintained my composure. After turning cautiously onto the high street, I retraced the route we'd taken into Old Cowerton. When the terraces came into view, Bree, who was acting as navigator, directed me to make a right turn onto Longview Lane.

As the map had indicated, Old Cowerton had erected three rows of six-unit row houses for its heroes. The swath of open parkland donated by the local farmer sloped upward to form a green and pleasant backdrop to the dull brown buildings. I cruised slowly past Parkview Terrace and Greenview Terrace, then turned right on Bellevue

Terrace, drinking in the details of a place that had once been as familiar to Annabelle Craven as Finch was to me.

The row houses weren't ugly, but they were joyless in their uniformity. Each was two stories tall and flat roofed, with a bay window on the ground floor and a shallow porch framing the front door. There were no front gardens. Instead, a narrow strip of lawn ran the length of each street, divided only by front walks that were, predictably, made of dull brown brick.

Though the back gardens were separated by dull brown-brick walls, they were as diverse as the buildings were uniform. If the residents of Bellevue Terrace chanced to look across the street into their neighbors' back gardens, they would be treated to the colorful sight of vegetable patches, flower beds, trellises, birdbaths, bird feeders, wind chimes, bicycles, abandoned toys, outdoor grills, an assortment of lawn furniture, two flagpoles, and one garishly painted totem pole.

"But no garages," I muttered, unsurprised.

I parked the Rover at the far end of Bellevue Terrace, in front of the row house Hayley Calthorp had identified as Annabelle's. It was a lonely spot, the last outpost of the terraces, beyond which there was nothing but overgrown grass and a tangle of wind-twisted trees. I saw no trace of the sign Annabelle had made when she'd christened her home Dovecote, but a wooden sign hanging above Minnie Jessop's front door told me that she'd dubbed her house Sunnyside.

"Sunnyside?" Bree said with a disparaging snort. "It should be called Gossipbottom."

A boxy blue sedan was parked in front of Sunnyside. It was one of the few cars I'd seen in the terraces. The absence of cars in such a remote location puzzled me until I remembered that it was Monday. The residents who had jobs had, of necessity, driven to them.

"Can you believe it, Lori?" Bree asked in awestruck tones. "We're here. We're actually here, at the scene of the crime."

"The alleged crime," I murmured, though I was equally awestruck.

"It doesn't look as though anyone's at home," Bree whispered. "No car out front. No lights in the windows."

"We're not breaking into Dovecote, Bree," I stated firmly.

"If they forgot to lock the front door, we wouldn't have to break in," she reasoned. "It wouldn't hurt to jiggle the doorknob, would it?"

"We're not sneaking into Dovecote, either," I said adamantly. "It's too late for sneaking. Once you've parked a canary-yellow Range Rover next door to Old Cowerton's gabbiest gossip, sneaking is no longer an option."

"I suppose you're right," Bree said with a regretful sigh.

"We'll walk casually around the side of the house and look into the back garden, as planned. Bess?" I said over my shoulder. "You ready to rumble?"

"Go!" she replied.

"You heard her," I said, releasing my seat belt. "Let's go! I'm not leaving before I see the rosebushes."

"Nor am I," said Bree, perking up.

The net curtains in Sunnyside's bay window twitched as we climbed out of the Rover. I was certain that Minnie Jessop was keeping an eye on us as I unfolded the pram and lowered Bess into it. Though I felt as if I had a pair of high-powered binoculars trained on me, I calmly fastened Bess's harness and moved on. I was too familiar with Finch's twitching curtains to let Minnie's rattle me.

"What a gloomy place to start married life," Bree commented, eyeing Annabelle's former home with distaste.

"Nonsense," I said, wheeling the pram into the long grass beside Dovecote. "It seems gloomy to you because you associate it with a gloomy tale. Annabelle probably felt like the luckiest girl in the world when she moved out of her parents' house and into her own."

"It has no character," Bree protested. "It looks as though it rolled off an assembly line."

"Doesn't matter," I told her. "Love makes the mundane magical."

"It would take more than love to make the terraces magical," Bree retorted, unconvinced. "A herd of unicorns might help, but I doubt it." She forged ahead of Bess and me to the rear of the house, where a brown brick wall enclosed Dovecote's back garden.

"Do *not* climb over the wall," I called to her.

"No breaking and entering, no trespassing," Bree grumbled. "You're no fun at all." She softened her words with a grin, stood on tiptoe to look over the garden wall, and gasped. "They're there, Lori! The rosebushes! They're at the end of the garden, just as Mrs. Craven said they would be, and they're enormous!"

My fearless daughter chortled gleefully as

159

I pushed the pram swiftly through a bumpy stretch of grass to catch up with Bree. When I reached her, I grasped the top of the wall with both hands and pulled myself onto my tiptoes to peer over it.

Compared to the terraces' other back gardens, Dovecote's was exceptionally tidy. A wrought-iron table and two wrought-iron chairs sat on a small brown-brick patio, facing a patch of lawn edged on two sides by long, narrow flower beds. The view from the patio would be spectacular in the summer, I thought, because the entire rear wall was covered from top to bottom by what Hayley Calthorp had described as the healthiest rosebushes in Old Cowerton.

It was too early in the year for blossoms, but I could easily envision what the bushes would look like in June. Their glossy leaves and their sturdy canes would have delighted the eye of the most exacting gardener, but my gaze was drawn inexorably to the dark, loamy soil covering their roots.

What else did the soil cover? I asked myself with an involuntary shiver. Were we gazing upon Zach Trotter's unmarked grave? I was about to hoist myself a little higher when a third question was asked, but not by me.

"May I help you?" said a voice.

TWELVE

Bree and I exchanged guilty glances, stepped away from the garden wall, and turned to face a woman standing knee deep in the grass near the front of the house, peering at us.

The woman wasn't old enough to be Minnie Jessop. Her graying hair suggested middle age, but her pageboy hairstyle and her slender build gave her a youthful air. She was dressed in a handsome tweed blazer, a button-down shirt, and pleated wool trousers. Though her arms were folded, she seemed to be amused rather than irate, as if she'd grown accustomed to catching strangers in the act of ogling Dovecote's notorious rosebushes.

"The house isn't for sale," she informed us.

"We're not house hunters," I told her. "We're, uh —"

"What Lori means," Bree interrupted, "is

that we're, er —"

The woman silenced our babbling with a wave of her hand.

"There's no need to explain," she said. "I know who you are." She gave us an appraising look, then wagged a beckoning finger at us. "Come along. My mother has been expecting you."

I gaped stupidly at her until Bree seized the pram's handles and treated Bess to another bouncy jaunt through the long grass. Bess's gurgling laughter brought me to my senses and I scrambled after them. The woman waited for me to complete our merry band, then introduced herself.

"I'm Susan Jessop," she said. "Unless I've been misinformed, you're Lori Shepherd and Bree Pym."

"And Bess Willis," I said, nodding at the pram. "My daughter."

"How do you do, Bess?" said Susan.

Bess mooed at her.

"Who told you about us?" I asked.

"I'll let Mother enlighten you," Susan said, with a glance at her wristwatch. "If I don't leave soon, I'll be late for work. I teach at the local agricultural college. My hours are flexible, but I try to set a good example for my students by getting to class on time."

She turned on her heel and strode across

Dovecote's lawn toward Sunnyside's front door. Bree looked as confused as I felt as we scurried after her.

"What do you teach?" Bree asked.

"Countryside management," Susan replied. "It involves —"

"Looking at how the countryside works," Bree broke in, "and how it can be managed to maximize benefits to wildlife, habitats, farmers, and recreational users." Noting Susan's perplexed gaze, she added, "My boyfriend is a conservationist. He talks a lot about countryside management."

"Good for him," said Susan, sounding impressed. "It's an important field of study in our crowded little island."

I felt a quiver of ghoulish anticipation as she walked ahead of us to open Sunnyside's front door. If Aunt Dimity was correct — and she usually was — Sunnyside's floor plan would be identical to Dovecote's. Once we stepped into Minnie Jessop's house, we would know if Annabelle Craven's story was plausible or if it was beyond the realm of possibility.

"May I bring Bess's pram inside?" I asked. "I'd rather not leave it outdoors, unattended."

"Feel free," Susan said. "If you like, you can wheel it through the house to the back

163

garden. Follow me."

I could scarcely believe my ears. It was as if Susan Jessop *wanted* me to reenact Zach Trotter's murder. I didn't know who or what awaited us in the back garden, but I knew a golden opportunity when I saw one. I thanked Susan and pushed the pram into a modest foyer, where I paused to examine my surroundings.

The wall to my right held a row of hooks from which dangled coats, hats, scarves, net shopping bags, and a lidless fishing creel that appeared to be a repository for mail. To my left, I could see the last few steps of an enclosed staircase that led, presumably, to the second floor. Ahead of me, a hallway led directly from the foyer to a room at the rear of the house.

"Straight shot," Bree said, just loud enough for me to know that her thoughts ran parallel to mine.

They were sickening thoughts, but I couldn't keep myself from thinking them. If Zach Trotter had tumbled down a similar staircase and landed in a similar foyer, it would have been child's play for Annabelle to drag his battered body through a similar hallway to the room closest to the back garden.

Feeling a little queasy, I pushed the pram

to the end of the hallway and into a surprisingly large and modern kitchen. Susan, who hadn't stopped to survey her own foyer, was already in the kitchen, holding the back door open for me.

"This way," she prompted.

I wheeled the pram toward her, all the while imagining how easy it would be to maneuver a fresh corpse around the kitchen table and over the door's low threshold to its final resting place. I was so absorbed in my macabre visions that it took a moment for me to register the strange tableau that met my eyes as I stepped into Sunnyside's sun-drenched garden.

Apart from a few wall-mounted wire baskets filled with sphagnum moss, the garden's only natural feature was a well-tended lawn. In the middle of the lawn sat a round glass-topped table surrounded by six plastic lawn chairs.

The table looked as though it had been set for afternoon tea, with six place settings, two creamers, two sugar bowls, a Victoria sponge cake, a stout plum cake, and several serving platters heaped with crustless sandwiches, cream buns, madeleines, meringues, petit fours, and the light-as-air confections known as Melting Moments, which were a great favorite of mine.

A tiny old woman in gold-rimmed spectacles was seated at the table, facing us. Despite the day's warmth, she was bundled up in a puffy jacket, a bobble cap, a plaid lap robe, and a pair of fingerless mittens. I tried not to stare at her, but it was hard to look away. I felt as if I'd been transported to an alternate universe in which afternoon tea was served at ten o'clock in the morning by a wizened gnome who'd mistaken a balmy day in April for a frigid day in February.

The woman had been talking on a cell phone when we entered the garden, but she slid the phone into her jacket pocket when Susan crossed to stand beside her.

"Here they are, Mum," Susan said. "I'll switch the kettle on before I leave. The teapot's on the kitchen table." She glanced at her watch again, then looked pleadingly from me to Bree. "Would one of you be kind enough to fill the pot when the kettle whistles? Mum isn't as steady on her feet as she used to be, and I really must dash. I'll see you later, Mum. Have a nice time."

Susan bent to kiss her mother's sunken cheek, then hurried back into the house. A moment later, I heard the front door open and close, followed by the sound of a car driving away from Sunnyside.

Though my head was in a whirl, my manners didn't desert me. I cleared my throat and said, "I'm very pleased to meet you, Mrs. Jessop."

"Call me Minnie," the old lady croaked, smiling toothlessly at us. Her lack of teeth gave her speech a sibilant quality, but she had no trouble making herself understood. "Bring that daughter of yours to me. I want to take a good look at her."

I lifted Bess from the pram and carried her to Minnie, but I didn't hand her over. I wasn't convinced that Minnie was strong enough to hold her.

"She's pretty as a princess," Minnie declared, shaking Bess's foot with a knobbly hand. "Healthy as a horse, too. Turn her loose. She won't come to any harm. The grass is warm and dry." She released Bess's foot and pointed a gnarled finger at the kitchen door. "You can fetch some saucepans for her to play with, if you like."

"Thanks, Minnie, but I brought toys for her to play with," I said, gesturing toward the diaper bag.

"Little ones prefer saucepans," Minnie said complacently. "I should know — I raised six of my own."

The kettle whistled.

"I'll get the tea," said Bree.

"The saucepans are in the cupboard next to the cooker," Minnie instructed her. "Don't forget the lids. Children love putting them on and taking them off again."

Bree nodded and retreated into the kitchen. I scanned the garden for hazards, detected none, and sat Bess on the lawn at a safe distance from the table and chairs. She seemed content to stay put while she explored the grass with her fingers, but I kept half an eye on her as I returned to Minnie's side.

"Are you expecting company?" I asked, surveying the six place settings.

"Just a few old friends," Minnie replied happily. "You and your chum are my guests of honor."

"We are?" I said, unenlightened.

Minnie patted the chair next to hers. "Take a seat, dear. I'll get a crick in my neck if I keep looking up at you, and at my age, cricks are a serious business."

I apologized for looming over her and lowered myself into the chair before asking the question I was burning to ask: "How did you know that Bree and I would be, um, available for your party?"

"Bob Nash rang me yesterday," Minnie explained. "Told me he'd had words with a daft Yank and a clueless Kiwi at the Willows.

Described that fancy pram of yours, too. Susan knew what to look for."

I brushed aside Bob Nash's curmudgeonly adjectives and reformulated my question. "But how did you and Susan know we'd come *here*? We didn't share our plans with Mr. Nash."

"My great-grandson Giles tipped me off," Minnie replied. "Giles is a florist. He looks after the plants at the White Hart."

In my mind's eye I saw a young man with a watering can going silently about his business in the White Hart's library.

"He overheard us talking to Francesco," I said as comprehension dawned.

"Giles is a good lad," Minnie said proudly. "When he heard you tell the Italian chap that you planned to visit Dovecote this morning, he rang me straightaway. He knew I'd want to meet you. My daughter Tina rang, too, after she saw you chatting with Hayley Calthorp in Nash's News."

A second image flitted across my mind.

"Does Tina wear a blue anorak?" I asked. "Did she go to Nash's News to buy travel supplies?"

"She's flying to Stockholm next week," Minnie informed me. "I hope she brings her anorak. It's bound to rain."

I sat back in my chair and regarded Minnie Jessop with a mixture of respect, admiration, and wariness. Minnie was no ordinary gossipmonger. She was a spymaster with a network of agents placed in strategic locations throughout Old Cowerton. Her slick operation made Finch's grapevine seem antiquated.

"Tea is served!" Bree announced.

She emerged from the kitchen carrying an oversized cobalt-blue teapot as well as a net shopping bag filled with saucepans and their attendant lids. She left the teapot on the table and emptied the bag in front of Bess. Bess didn't need any tips on what to do with the saucepans, but Bree played with her for a few minutes before returning to claim the chair next to mine.

"One of you will have to be Mother," said Minnie. She gazed ruefully at her twisted hands. "I can't lift the big teapot anymore."

"Allow me," I said, and filled our cups.

"Susan and I did the baking last night," said Minnie, "but we made the sandwiches fresh this morning. Go ahead, help yourselves."

I could almost hear the Melting Moments call to me, but it seemed impolite to sample them before the rest of Minnie's guests arrived. Bree, on the other hand, didn't hesitate to reach for a cream bun. Minnie eyed her approvingly, then got down to brass tacks.

"Is it true that you know Annabelle Craven?" she asked.

"It is," I replied. "She's a good friend of ours."

Minnie patted my arm consolingly. "You're not to blame, and so I told Bob Nash. Annabelle always was a charmer. I'm sure Hayley Calthorp told you that I made up hateful stories about Annabelle, but *I know what I saw.*"

"What did you see?" Bree asked eagerly.

Minnie opened her mouth to speak, then cupped a hand around her ear to catch the sound of a vehicle pulling up in front of Sunnyside. A moment later, the doorbell rang.

"Oh, good," she said, grinning gappily. "They're here."

THIRTEEN

Bree stifled a frustrated groan and volunteered to answer the door. As she darted into the house, Minnie withdrew a set of dentures from the pocket of her puffy jacket and inserted them into her mouth.

"I hate wearing my teeth," she told me, after poking them into position, "but I can't chew properly without them."

I didn't know what to say, so I confined myself to a sympathetic nod. Bess had switched from the lid-on, lid-off game to the bang-a-lid-on-a-random-saucepan game. The noise seemed to delight Minnie, but I found her toothy grin faintly menacing.

I was beginning to think that Bree had gotten lost on her way to the front door when she returned, trailed by three elderly women, each of whom walked at a snail's pace with the aid of a three-pronged metal cane. Like Minnie, the newcomers were dressed as if they were on a polar expedition, though their jackets were noticeably shabbier than hers. When they caught sight of Bess, they began slowly but surely to converge on her.

"They love to play with saucepans," one of the women observed in a quavering voice, and the other two croaked their agreement.

When Bess saw three three-pronged canes and six legs moving toward her, she let out a cry of alarm. I jumped to my feet, skirted the oncoming traffic, lifted her from the ground, and introduced her to the ancient trio. Freed from the fear of being simultaneously trampled and skewered, Bess accepted their praise with aplomb until the tasty treats on the table reminded her — and me — that lunchtime was nigh.

"Minnie," I said to our hostess, "I'm afraid Bess needs her lunch. I don't mean to be unsociable, but would you mind if she ate it in the kitchen? She'll be too distracted to eat if I feed her out here."

"You go ahead." Minnie tilted her head toward the three old ladies. "It'll take a while to organize this lot. They don't get out much."

"Bring the pram, will you, Bree?" I said, giving her a meaningful look. "Bess can nap in it after she has her lunch."

Bree took her cue and wheeled the pram into the kitchen. I gently withdrew Bess from her circle of admirers and followed in Bree's footsteps, making sure to close the door behind me. I didn't want to run the risk being overheard again.

Bess sat in my lap to gorge herself on the buffet I'd packed for her, but Bree prowled the room like a caged tiger, talking sometimes to herself and sometimes to me.

"Did you see the staircase, Lori?" she asked. "Did you see the hallway? Annabelle could have hauled a morgueful of corpses into the garden without breaking a sweat. How did Minnie know you'd spoken with Hayley Calthorp? How did Susan know we'd come here? How did she know our names? What's with the tea party? Who are those old ladies? The van from the local nursing home dropped them off, but I don't know why they'd want to meet us. *What's going on?*"

"Are you done?" I asked when she stopped prowling.

"For the moment," she answered, and sank into the chair opposite mine.

"I admit that Sunnyside's layout makes Mrs. Craven's story seem less bonkers than it did before," I conceded, "but I still don't think we should jump to any conclusions."

"The jump's getting shorter and shorter," Bree muttered.

"As for how Susan knew our names . . ." I filled her in on Minnie's spy network, concluding with Bob Nash's pithy description of us as "a daft Yank and a clueless Kiwi."

Bree chuckled in spite of herself. "Perfect! We should print business cards for ourselves: The Daft and Clueless Detective Agency."

"Wouldn't it send the wrong message to our clients?" I asked.

"Probably not," she said. "I'm still clueless about the old ladies."

"My guess is that they're the women Hayley Calthorp talked about," I said, "the ones she called Minnie's cronies. I'll bet Minnie invited them here for moral support. She knows we've heard Hayley's side of the story and she wants us to hear hers. She must be desperate to convince us — or anyone else who will listen — that she's been right about Annabelle all along."

"But why have a tea party?" Bree asked.

"Kindness?" I replied, catching a wheat cracker before it hit the floor. "Didn't you notice? Every treat on the tea table is easy to chew. It seems to me that Minnie made them because she and her chums have the same dental challenges. And you heard what she said. Her friends don't get out much."

Bree nodded gravely. "A nursing home tea party probably isn't as much fun as a tea party at a friend's house."

"Probably not," I said.

Bree lapsed into silence, then said quietly, "It's a lot to take in."

"No kidding," I said. "And there's more to come. If I'm right, we're about to hear the gospel according to Minnie."

After her busy morning, Bess didn't need much encouragement to fall asleep in her pram. I wheeled her close to the kitchen doorway, where I could keep her in view and at the same time insulate her from the hubbub of conversation and cackling laughter in the garden.

At least one of Minnie's cronies must have been strong enough to lift the big teapot because the tea party was well under way. By the time Bree and I resumed our seats at the glass-topped table, the ladies had dispatched half of the sandwiches, most of the plum cake, and, to my disappointment, every last one of the Melting Moments. Their speedy demolition of Minnie's offerings made me wonder if they got enough to eat at the nursing home.

Minnie waited for us to be seated, then took charge of the introductions. The woman wearing a fine hair net over her sparse white curls was Mildred Greenham. The woman with a bulky hearing aid in each ear was Mabel Parson. The woman with the hunched back was Myrtle Black.

"Mildred," "Mabel," and "Myrtle," I recalled, were the names Annabelle preferred to her own. I wondered if these were the girls who'd teased her in the school yard because her mother had wanted her to stand out from the other children.

"I told my chums about your friendship with Annabelle Craven," Minnie informed us.

"Minnie rang us yesterday," said Mildred, "after Bob Nash, Giles, and Tina rang her."

"You don't want to believe everything Hayley Calthorp tells you," Mabel advised. "We came along to set the record straight."

Myrtle chuckled. "I'll bet Hayley had some choice things to say about you, Minnie."

"I'm sure she did," Minnie said unflappably. She was clearly the queen bee in her small circle. "But it's not her fault. She's only parroting what her gran told her, and her gran was as gullible as a newborn babe."

The cronies nodded, and Minnie turned

her head to face us.

"What I'm about to tell you is God's own truth," she said solemnly. "Hayley Calthorp believes differently, but I know what I saw."

"It was a moonless night," said Myrtle.

"I'll tell my own story, thank you very much," Minnie snapped. "You'll have your turn later."

"Get on with it, then," Myrtle retorted, transferring a thick slice of Victoria sponge to her plate. "At the rate you're going, we'll be here until Christmas."

"My story begins *before* the moonless night," Minnie explained, turning her back on Myrtle and fastening her attention on Bree and me. "It began before the children came along, a few months after my husband and I were married. We thought it would be nice to live next door to another pair of newlyweds, but it wasn't. The Trotters weren't the kind of neighbors we'd hoped for."

"No one would want to live next door to Zach Trotter," said Mildred, unknowingly echoing Hayley Calthorp's comment about living next door to Minnie Jessop.

"He was a bad lot," Minnie stated firmly, "a liar, a drinker, and a brawler. My husband and I got used to hearing him come home at all hours, drunk as a lord. He never raised his hand to Annabelle, but he raised his voice, and the things he said to her don't bear repeating."

The cronies nodded sadly.

"No one would have blamed Annabelle for leaving him," Minnie opined, "but she stuck by him until —"

"The moonless night," Myrtle put in excitedly.

"Yes, Myrtle, it *was* a moonless night," Minnie said, glaring at her old friend. She gathered herself, then went on. "My husband and I were in the front parlor, drinking a cup of cocoa before bed. We were just finishing up when we heard Zach Trotter come home. We could tell by the way he fumbled with his latch key that he was sozzled."

"As usual," Myrtle mumbled through a mouthful of Victoria sponge.

"We heard him go upstairs," Minnie went on, "and a little while later, we heard a dreadful noise — a sort of bump-thud-rumbling noise. We were sure Zach had fallen down the stairs."

"Why not Annabelle?" I asked.

"Annabelle was a slip of a girl," said Minnie. "If she'd fallen down the stairs, she wouldn't have made half as much noise as a big chap like Zach."

"Makes sense," Bree allowed.

"Of course it does," Minnie said irritably. "It's what happened."

"What did you do after you heard the terrible noise?" I asked, to keep Minnie from biting Bree's head off.

"Nothing," Minnie answered. "We reckoned that if Zach was bad hurt, Annabelle would ring for the doctor. If he wasn't, we'd see him all bruised the next day."

"And serve him right!" Mabel said fiercely.

"We waited up for a bit," Minnie continued, "to see if the doctor would come. When he didn't, my husband went up to bed and I took our empty cups to rinse in the kitchen. I was in the back garden when I heard —"

"Why were you in the back garden?" Bree interrupted.

The cronies tittered. Minnie gave them a withering look, then turned toward Bree.

"Why do you think I was in the back garden?" she asked tartly. "We didn't have modern conveniences in those days." She pointed to the kitchen's rear wall. "The WC used to be right there, behind the scullery. We got rid of it when we expanded the kitchen — *after* we installed the indoor loo."

"Oh, I see," said Bree, blushing crimson. "Sorry."

"As I was saying," Minnie resumed, "I was in the back garden when I heard a queer sound coming from over the wall." She waved a mittened hand at the brick wall separating her garden from Dovecote's. "I was afraid it might be burglars, so I stood on an upturned bucket to take a look. And what do you think I saw?"

Her cronies seemed to hold their collective breath.

"Not much," Bree said irrepressibly. "It was a moonless night."

Myrtle sniggered, but Minnie ignored her.

"The stars were plenty bright enough to see by," she assured Bree. "And I saw Annabelle, plain as day, in her dressing gown and gum boots, tipping a rolled-up rug into the trench she'd dug for her roses."

An unpleasant sense of recognition made the hairs on the back of my neck rise. Minnie's description of the rolled-up rug and the trench matched Annabelle's exactly.

"It was the rag rug she made special for her foyer, wasn't it, Minnie?" said Mildred.

"It was," Minnie confirmed. "She shoveled a bit of soil into the trench to cover up the rug, then went back into the house. The next morning, she planted her roses. When I called on her later in the day to borrow a cup of sugar, the rag rug was nowhere to be seen. She made up some tale about Zach abandoning her, but she and I knew what she'd done." Minnie took a deep breath and concluded dramatically, "Like I told the police: I heard Zach Trotter come home that night, but I never saw him leave."

Bree, who was much braver than I, said, "Hayley Calthorp believes Annabelle's story."

"Did Hayley see what I saw?" Minnie demanded. "No, she did not! Her gran had a soft spot for Annabelle, and Annabelle took advantage of it, just like she took advantage of that bird-witted constable who came to question her. Why they sent such a dunderhead to investigate a murder, I'll never know. He couldn't see past her blue eyes and blond curls."

"Be fair," Myrtle protested. "The police had their hands full with the robbery at St. Leonard's."

"The robbery that never happened," Minnie scoffed. "It was a false alarm, but it kept the police from sending their best men to look into Zach Trotter's murder. I told that fool of a constable what I saw, but he seemed to think the rag rug walked away by itself. He didn't even open his notebook, much less dig up the roses. He let Annabelle twist him round her little finger. Just like the others."

"The others?" Bree and I chorused. Bree's arrested expression told me that she, too, remembered Francesco's mysterious words.

"There were bound to be others," said Minnie. "A curse came upon her the moment she pushed her husband down the stairs. The only way she could free herself from it was to stop pretending that she was a helpless, abandoned wife and to confess that she was a widow — a self-made, murderous widow."

"Which she never did," said Myrtle.

"The widow's curse blackened her heart and twisted her mind," Minnie continued. "Annabelle may have had the face of an angel, but she had the soul of a devil." After an ominous pause, Minnie pointed at Mildred and said affably, "Your turn, dear."

FOURTEEN

Mildred Greenham seemed to be in no hurry to take her turn. She wiped a smear of cream from her lips with a cloth napkin, took a long sip of tea, and patted her thinning hair, as if to reassure herself that her hair net was still in place, before she turned her rheumy gaze on Bree and me.

"Annabelle Trotter may have evaded the law," she said portentously, "but she could not escape the widow's curse."

A lonely cloud drifted across the sun and the temperature seemed to plunge. The old ladies' shadowed faces seemed suddenly sinister. A shiver would have slithered down my spine if Myrtle's querulous voice hadn't broken the mood.

"Oh, stop showing off," she scolded as the sun came out of hiding.

"I'm not showing off," Mildred protested.

"Yes, you are," Myrtle insisted. "There's no sense in bringing up the widow's curse *now.*"

"Minnie brought it up first," Mildred pointed out.

"Yes, but she was *introducing* it," said Myrtle. "You're putting things back to front."

"Myrtle's right," Minnie agreed. "They'll think we're batty if you tell things out of order, Mildred."

"It's Minnie, then you, then Myrtle, then me," Mabel said to Mildred, ticking the names off on her fingers. "Then we all tell the last bit, but I get to tell most of it because of my cousin Florence."

The old friends bickered among themselves for a few more minutes before Mildred caved in to peer pressure.

"All right," she grumbled. "I'll say my piece and let you say yours."

"I should think so," said Mabel, eyeing Mildred indignantly.

Mildred took another sip of tea and started again. "Before I was married, I worked as a receptionist at the Old Cowerton Dairy. A young man named Ted Fletcher worked there, too."

"Hayley Calthorp told me about Ted Fletcher's accident," I said hastily, hoping to head off a graphic account of his dreadful death. "She also told me that Annabelle and Ted were good friends."

"Good friends." Minnie clucked her tongue scornfully. "It's just the sort of mealymouthed rubbish I'd expect to hear from Hayley. The truth is, Annabelle set her cap at Ted Fletcher."

"Annabelle wanted to move up in the world, didn't she?" said Myrtle. "Wanted a husband with a steady job. Wanted one who didn't spend his pay packet at the pub."

"It's what we all wanted," Mabel acknowledged, "but we went about it in the right way."

"I warned Ted about Annabelle, but he wouldn't listen to me," Minnie said. "He couldn't see past her blue eyes and blond curls."

"He adored her," said Mabel. "Couldn't do enough for her. He was always stopping by to oil a squeaky hinge or to hang a picture for her."

"Annabelle didn't know a hammer from a spanner," Minnie said bluntly.

Everyone jumped as Mildred rapped the table with her knuckles.

"I beg your pardon," she said heatedly. "Is it my turn or not?"

Chastened, Minnie, Myrtle, and Mabel apologized to Mildred and nodded for her to go on.

"My desk faced the big windows in the front office," she explained, redirecting her attention to Bree and me. "It was part of my job to keep an eye on everyone who came and went at the dairy."

An ideal position, I thought, for one of Minnie's inquisitive cronies.

"On the fatal day," Mildred continued, "I saw Ted Fletcher walk toward the slurry pit. But he wasn't the only one I saw." She paused dramatically, as if awaiting a response.

Bree obliged. "Who else did you see, Mildred?"

"Annabelle Trotter!" she replied triumphantly. "I saw her as clearly as I see you. I watched her come up the dairy's drive and follow Ted to the slurry pit." Her eyes narrowed as she added, "She was carrying a picnic hamper."

"She was carrying a picnic hamper to a slurry pit?" I said doubtfully, recalling Aunt Dimity's remarks about poisonous fumes. "Seems like an odd place for a picnic."

"A very odd place," Mildred agreed. "The next thing I knew, there was running and shouting and the whole dairy was in an uproar. Poor Ted had been missed, you see, and the head cowman had found him floating facedown in the slurry. They pulled poor

Ted out and tried to revive him, but it was too late." She sighed heavily. "The kiss of life can't save a dead man."

I set aside a half-eaten madeleine and tried not to replay the image Mildred had conjured in my mind.

"The coroner ruled it an accidental death," Mildred continued, "but there was nothing accidental about it."

"Hold on," said Bree, frowning. "Are you suggesting that Annabelle *pushed* Ted Fletcher into the slurry pit?"

"There were no eyewitnesses," Mildred allowed, "but it was easy enough to put two and two together."

"It's not easy for me," Bree said. "Why would Annabelle kill a man who adored her?"

"Why would she bring a picnic hamper to a slurry pit?" Mildred asked in return. "Because she needed an excuse to go there. Why did she need an excuse? Because she wanted to get rid of Ted Fletcher."

"By then, a cowhand wasn't good enough for her," Minnie interjected. "She'd set her sights on someone higher up the social ladder."

"But why would she murder Ted?" Bree pressed. "There are less drastic ways to break up with a guy."

"Not for Annabelle," said Minnie. "Her mind was poisoned by the widow's curse. You'll see."

"My turn!" Myrtle chirped.

"Go ahead, dear," Mildred said graciously, popping another cream puff into her mouth.

Myrtle's deep-set eyes shone with a gossip's gleam. Considering the dark turn our conversation had taken, the gleam seemed a bit out of place, but it was familiar to me. I'd seen it in my neighbors' eyes often enough, just as they'd seen it in mine.

"There's no moonless night in my story," Myrtle began. "Mine happened in broad daylight, about a year after Ted Fletcher died." She rested her forearms on the table, as if to relieve the strain on her hunched back. "It started when Annabelle took on sewing work for the big house."

"The big house?" I queried.

"The manor house," Myrtle clarified.

"Halfway up the valley on the other side of town?" I said, envisioning the enclosed property I'd noticed as we'd driven toward Old Cowerton from the Oxford road.

"That's right," said Myrtle. "They always had work for Annabelle at the big house — repairing tapestries and damask tablecloths and other fancy stuff."

"Say what you will about Annabelle,"

Mildred commented, "she was an expert needlewoman. The vicar wouldn't let anyone else mend his vestments, and you could scarcely see her stitches when she repaired the town hall's flag after the windstorm shredded it."

The other ladies began to voice their views on Annabelle Craven's sewing skills, but Myrtle cleared her throat peremptorily and they subsided.

"Annabelle was in and out of the big house all the time, picking up projects or dropping them off," Myrtle continued. "She had to walk there because she couldn't afford a motorcar. That's how she met Jim Salford."

"Poor Jim," Mabel murmured.

"Jim was the gamekeeper at the manor house," Myrtle explained. "Annabelle met him one day when she was walking up the drive. He was a big, strapping fellow, as good-looking as you please and more dashing than any cowman."

"I'll wager he smelled better, too," said Mildred.

"I'll wager he did, but there's no need to say it out loud," Myrtle scolded. "The main thing to remember is: Jim made more money than Ted." She raised her hands, palms upward. "Why would Annabelle settle for a cowman when she could have a handsome, well-paid gamekeeper?" She folded her arms on the table again and shrugged dismissively. "Oh, she let a few months go by after Ted Fletcher's death, for appearances' sake, but all the while she had her sights set on poor Jim." She shook her head. "He never stood a chance."

"Blue eyes, blond curls," murmured Minnie.

"Jim fell for her, hook, line, and sinker," Myrtle said with a puckish smirk.

Her friends chuckled appreciatively, but I didn't get the joke.

"What's so funny?" Bree asked.

"What's funny is, Jim really did fall for her, hook, line, and sinker," said Myrtle. "Jim was teaching Annabelle how to fish when he fell into the river and drowned."

"No," I said, aghast. "Not another drowning."

"And another fall," said Myrtle. "It makes you think, doesn't it?"

"It must have been terrible for Annabelle," I said.

"It was worse for Jim," Myrtle pointed out.

"I warned him," Minnie intoned.

"Jim's death was ruled accidental as well," Myrtle informed us, "but since Annabelle was the only eyewitness, who knows what really happened?"

"We do," said Mabel.

"Let me guess," Bree said, with the faintest hint of sarcasm in her voice. "Annabelle had set her sights on another man."

Myrtle gave Mabel a significant nod. "Your turn, dear. Tell them about William Walker."

Mabel made a small adjustment to her hearing aids, then sat up primly and launched into her part of the story. "William Walker's full name was William Walker May, but we called him William Walker on account of his dad being known as William."

"We have the same problem in my family," I told her. "Too many Williams."

"We have too many Richards in ours," Myrtle piped up. "Richard, Rich, Dick, Dickie —"

"That's as may be," Mabel interrupted impatiently, "but I'm talking about William Walker, so you can be quiet about your Richards." She folded her veined and knotted hands and carried on. "William Walker was as fine a man as ever you'll meet. He wasn't as dashing as Jim Salford, but he was well-spoken and dignified. Never a hair out of place, always a crease in his trousers. When his dad retired, William Walker was ready to step into his shoes."

"What did his dad do?" Bree inquired.

"He was the butler in the big house," Mabel replied.

"I'll bet William Walker May made more money than Jim Salford," Bree said drily.

"He made lots more," Mabel confirmed, "and he was a step up the ladder, so to speak."

"Why would Annabelle settle for a game-keeper when she could have a butler?" Bree asked.

"She wouldn't," said Mabel. "She caught William Walker's eye while she was still seeing Jim. Chatted him up, bold as brass."

"How do you know?" Bree asked.

"My cousin Florence was a live-in parlor maid at the big house," Mabel answered. "Not much went on there without her knowing about it. She saw Annabelle draw William Walker in."

"I imagine you warned William Walker," Bree said to Minnie.

"I did," she said sorrowfully, "but he —"

"Wouldn't listen," Bree finished for her. "Blond hair? Blue eyes?"

"William Walker grew Amazon lilies as a hobby," Mabel said, taking back the reins of her tale. "Won blue ribbons for them at the flower show. When he took over his dad's

193

job at the big house, they let him have a little greenhouse all to himself. On his days off, he brought Annabelle there." She leaned forward until her chin was nearly touching what was left of the Victoria sponge, her keen eyes fixed on Bree's face. "One winter's day, just over a year after Jim Salford's death, William Walker went into his little greenhouse and *died.*"

"Did he drown?" Bree inquired with a transparently false air of innocence.

"In a manner of speaking," said Mabel, undeterred by Bree's tone. "The coroner ruled that the heater in the greenhouse malfunctioned. William Walker died of carbon monoxide poisoning." She tapped the table with a finger as she added, "He *suffocated.*"

"Which is a lot like drowning," Mildred pointed out helpfully.

"Can you guess who was at the big house on the day William Walker died?" Mabel asked. Instead of waiting for a reply, she tapped the table again and exclaimed, "Annabelle Trotter!"

"You can't think that she —" I began, outraged, but my protest was cut short by a soft moo.

Bess was awake.

FIFTEEN

It was just as well that Bess woke when she did. I needed a break from the tea party. Though I did not for one moment believe in the widow's curse, the litany of deaths connected to Annabelle Craven had unsettled me. The deaths of even two suitors would have been tragic and terribly unlucky . . . but *three*? What were the odds?

While it was true that Minnie seemed to be enjoying herself a bit too much, her eyewitness account of Annabelle burying the rug was virtually identical to the story Annabelle had shared with me. Then, too, there were the unavoidable implications of Sunnyside's floor plan. I was no longer certain that Hayley Calthorp's version of events was the only one worth considering.

Since Sunnyside wasn't furnished with toddlers in mind, I used the Rover's cargo area as a changing table. It wasn't the first time I'd done so, nor was it the first time that my daughter's smile had soothed my troubled mind. When I carried her back to the garden, I thought I was ready to take whatever Minnie and her cronies could throw at me. Unfortunately, I was mistaken.

After the cronies had cooed and billowed over Bess, I left her, Moo, and a few favorite toys among the saucepans and reclaimed my place at the table.

"Did I miss anything?" I asked brightly.

"I made a fresh pot of tea," said Bree, "and Minnie gave me her recipe for Melting Moments."

"Bree told us about her young man as well," Minnie informed me.

"We told her to marry him," said Mildred.

"What did she say to that?" I asked, grinning.

"She told us to mind our own business," Myrtle said admiringly. "You're a pistol, Bree!"

"It takes one to know one," said Bree, bowing to Myrtle.

"Well," I said, nodding cordially at the old ladies, "it's been an interesting and informative, uh, get-together. Thanks for taking the time to —"

"We're not done yet," Minnie interrupted.

"You're not?" I said weakly.

"Far from it," she said. "We've saved the

worst for last."

My heart sank as I murmured, "Oh, goody."

Minnie had evidently eaten her fill because she removed her teeth, swirled them in her water glass, and wiped them dry with a napkin. After slipping them into her pocket, she smacked her lips a few times, as if savoring her liberation.

"You may be wondering," she said, "why Annabelle got rid of William Walker."

"Something tells me that there was another man on her horizon," said Bree. She put a hand to her brow like a psychic receiving a message from the Great Beyond. "A man who earned more than William Walker, who was higher up the social ladder, and who couldn't see past her blond hair and blue eyes, despite your warnings." She dropped her hand and raised her eyebrows expectantly. "Am I close?"

"You're spot-on," Minnie responded.

"The man was Edwin Craven," said Myrtle.

"Edwin Craven stood on the top rung of the social ladder in Old Cowerton," said Minnie, "and he was as rich as Croesus."

"He was the lord of the manor," said Mildred.

"He wasn't the real lord," Myrtle interjected. "The real lord sold the manor to Mr. Craven and moved to Majorca."

"Craven Manor it was called after that," said Mildred, "though old folks like us still call it the big house."

"Or the manor," Myrtle put in.

Mabel, who'd been munching on a meringue, hastened to get in on the act.

"My cousin Florence," she said, spraying meringue crumbs far and wide, "was hoovering the carpet in the morning room when William Walker introduced Annabelle to Mr. Craven. She couldn't hear what they were saying, but she could see them standing together near the grand staircase in the front hall."

"Poor William Walker sealed his own fate when he introduced Annabelle to Edwin," Mildred said dolorously.

"Once Annabelle met Edwin, she had to have him," said Minnie.

"She couldn't have anyone else," said Myrtle. "By then, no other man in Old Cowerton would go near her."

"They were afraid they'd end up like Ted Fletcher, Jim Salford, and William Walker May," Mildred elucidated, in case Bree and I had missed the point.

"Was Edwin Craven aware of Annabelle's, um, track record?" I asked awkwardly.

"Of course he was," said Minnie. "When I heard he'd taken a liking to her, I marched up to the big house and told him to watch his step." She shook her head. "I may as well have saved my breath. He was too far gone by then to pay attention to anything I said."

"He couldn't marry Annabelle right away," said Myrtle, "but the moment a judge declared Zach Trotter dead, he whisked her off to St. Leonard's."

"It was a quiet wedding, I'll give her that," Mildred allowed, toying with her teacup. "Though how she could stand up in church and say her marriage vows with three head-stones and an unmarked grave to her name is past understanding."

"I'm surprised Edwin lived long enough to marry her," said Bree, with a coy, sidelong glance at Minnie.

"So were we," said Minnie.

"She had what she wanted, didn't she?" said Myrtle. "She was the lady of the manor. She didn't have to scrimp and save anymore. She didn't have to make her own clothes or clean her own house or hem dresses for a living."

"She had servants to wait on her and more jewelry than was good for her," said Mildred. "She traveled all over the world with

Mr. Craven, and she mixed with his family and friends, but she kept well clear of the town."

"She knew we were watching her," said Mabel. "She knew we were waiting for the curse to catch up with her."

"It took longer than we expected," said Minnie, "but she did him in, in the end."

"She did him in?" I repeated, nonplussed. "Annabelle told me that Edwin died of Alzheimer's disease."

"He had Alzheimer's," Minnie acknowledged, "but it was the widow's curse that killed him."

"She kept him at home for the first year or so," said Mabel. "Then she put him into a nursing home."

"Your nursing home?" Bree asked.

Her question provoked an outburst of hearty laughter.

"We're at Newhaven," said Mildred, after the laughter died away. "Newhaven wasn't posh enough to suit Annabelle. She put Edwin in Cloverhill, over by Tewkesbury."

"Cloverhill has an indoor swimming pool," Mabel said dreamily, "and a riding stable and a garden and painting classes and yoga and concerts and a full-time staff of specialist doctors and nurses."

"We're lucky if we see a doctor once a

200

month," said Mildred.

"We're lucky if we can get someone to clean the toilets," Myrtle grumbled.

I ducked my head, too embarrassed by my many blessings to look the old ladies in the eye.

"It sounds as if Annabelle was doing everything she could for Edwin," said Bree.

"It appeared that way," Minnie agreed, "until she went against his doctor's advice and brought him home from Cloverhill for an overnight visit. She hired a private nurse to look after him, but —"

"Stop right there," Mabel interrupted. "I get to tell this part, on account of my cousin Florence."

"So you do," Minnie said amiably. "I beg your pardon."

Mabel straightened her shoulders and lifted her chin, as if she were the star witness at a trial. "Florence had a bedsit on the top floor in Craven Manor, but she didn't have her own kitchen. If she wanted a snack between meals, she had to fetch it from the big kitchen downstairs, at the back of the house." She peered from Bree to me and asked, "With me so far?"

"Florence upstairs, kitchen downstairs," said Bree. "Got it."

"On the night Annabelle brought Edwin

home from Cloverhill, Florence felt restless," Mabel continued. "She'd been run off her feet all day, getting a room ready for him and the hired nurse, and she couldn't settle. She thought a cup of warm milk might help, so she went down to the kitchen to make one."

"Very sensible," said Mildred. "Warm milk always sends me off."

"I prefer hot chocolate," said Minnie.

"A hot toddy works for me," Myrtle declared. "Wish we could have hot toddies at Newhaven."

"I'll bet Cloverhill's residents can have as many hot toddies as they like," Mildred said with a wistful sigh.

"Florence was in the kitchen," Mabel reiterated, raising her voice, "when she heard a horrible noise in the front hall."

"It was the same noise my husband and I heard the night Zach Trotter died," Minnie put in. "A bump-thud-rumbling noise."

"The very same," Mabel confirmed. "Florence ran to the front hall as fast as ever she could, and when she got there, she saw the most awful sight: Edwin Craven was sprawled on the floor at the bottom of the grand staircase, and he was as dead as a doornail. Florence told me he looked like a broken doll, with his arms and legs flung

202

every which way and his neck bent all funny and his wide-open eyes staring up at the big chandelier."

"Poor Edwin," Mildred murmured. "Another headstone at St. Leonard's."

"And there was Annabelle," Mabel went on, "standing on the landing at the top of the stairs. Her hands were balled into fists and her chest was heaving, and before she started screaming, Florence swears she saw a flicker of relief cross her face, as if she'd finally done what she'd wanted to do all along. All Florence could think of was Dr. Jekyll and Mr. Hyde, so she ran back to the kitchen and hid in the scullery until the police came."

"Where was the hired nurse?" Bree asked.

"She was sound asleep on the easy chair in Edwin's room," Mabel replied.

"She fell asleep on the job?" Bree said, sounding scandalized.

"She did, and she was struck off for it, but it wasn't her fault," said Mabel. "Annabelle drugged her."

"She . . . *what*?" I said, certain that I'd misheard her.

"Annabelle drugged the nurse," Mabel said. "There were sleeping tablets on Edwin's night table when Florence dusted it that afternoon, but they were gone when the police came."

"Annabelle slipped them into the nurse's coffee," said Myrtle. "It was the only way she could keep the nurse from putting a stop to her wicked plan."

"She waited until the nurse passed out," said Mabel. "Then she got Edwin out of bed, led him to the landing, and pushed him down the stairs. Florence told the police about the sleeping pills and the look on Annabelle's face, but they ignored her. She handed in her notice the next day."

"The inquest ended with the usual verdict," said Minnie, "but Edwin Craven's death was no more an accident than Zach's, Ted's, Jim's, and William Walker's. Annabelle did away with all of them."

"We reckon they came back to haunt her," said Myrtle. "That's why she left Craven Manor."

"A guilty conscience can cope with one or two ghosts," Mildred informed us, "but five is too many."

"Have any men died accidentally in your village since Annabelle came to live there?" Minnie inquired, turning to Bree and me.

"No," I replied. "Not one."

"It's only a matter of time," Minnie said serenely. "There's no escaping the widow's curse."

Sixteen

The nursing home van collected Mildred, Myrtle, and Mabel at half past two. Minnie sent them off with a shopping bag filled with treats she and Susan had baked especially for them. I hoped fervently that the homemade cookies and cakes would make life a little less bleak for them at Newhaven.

Bree and I offered to clear the table, but Minnie declined.

"A fine hostess I'd be if I made my guests of honor clean up after themselves," she scolded. "Susan will tidy up when she comes home." She squinted skyward. "It's time for you to take that daughter of yours back to the White Hart. The house will block the sun in a little while, and it'll get chilly out here. You don't want Bess to come down with the sniffles."

Minnie insisted on accompanying us to the front door, pausing only to present us with a goody bag she took from the kitchen counter. When we reached the foyer, she nodded at the bag.

"You'll find some of my Melting Moments in there," she said, smiling slyly at me. "I saw your face fall when you thought we'd eaten the lot."

"I've never been much of a poker player," I admitted sheepishly. "Are you sure you don't want us to stay with you until Susan comes home?"

"There's no need," she assured me. "I've said all I have to say. What you do with it is up to you." She shook a gnarled finger at us. "You can't say you weren't warned!"

She caressed Bess's silky curls and chucked Moo under the chin, then opened the door. Bree led the way to the Rover. We loaded it in silence while Minnie watched from the doorway. She gave us a cheerful wave as we drove away and we waved back, but I was still worried about leaving her on her own. To my relief, we passed Susan's boxy blue sedan heading into the terraces as we were heading out.

As we turned onto the main road, Bree burst out laughing.

"Farewell to the Sunnyside Gang," she said. "Farewell to Minnie's house of horrors." She shook her head, still grinning. "What a big bucket of nonsense. If you ask me, Minnie and her cronies have been skipping their meds."

"I take it you have doubts about their veracity," I said drily.

"I'd have doubts about anyone who was crackbrained enough to believe in curses and ghosts," Bree scoffed.

I thought of the blue journal and suppressed a smile.

"Besides," she continued, "their stories were as full of holes as a cheese grater."

"Show me the holes," I said.

"Ted Fletcher was a professional cowman," Bree stated. "He wouldn't let a girl he adored come anywhere near a slurry pit. Can you picture him and Annabelle enjoying a romantic picnic next to a poo pond? It's ludicrous."

"And Jim?" I asked.

"Gamekeepers have accidents," Bree said simply. "A knife slips, a shotgun goes off prematurely, a branch falls after a windstorm. . . . I have a lot less trouble believing that Jim Salford slipped on a mossy rock and fell into the river than I have believing that Annabelle shoved him."

"William Walker?" I prompted, reassured by her certainty.

"If Annabelle didn't know a spanner from a hammer," Bree argued, "how could she sabotage the heater in William Walker's greenhouse?"

"What about the look of relief Florence saw on Annabelle's face after Edwin's fatal fall?" I asked.

"Alzheimer's is a bloody awful disease," said Bree. "I'd be heartbroken if someone I loved suffered from it. If an accident put an end to the suffering, I wouldn't be at all surprised if I felt a tiny flicker of relief mixed in with my grief and horror. I might not admit it, even to myself, but I'd probably feel it."

"The drugged nurse?" I pressed.

"Mabel's cousin Florence didn't actually see Annabelle slip the sleeping tablets into the nurse's coffee," Bree reminded me. "It's much more likely that the nurse gave them to Edwin to help him sleep."

"So the nurse nodded off without Annabelle's assistance," I said.

"Nurses who work night shifts have been known to fall asleep on duty," said Bree. "It's a shame, but it happens."

I fell silent for a moment, then said, "Wait a minute. You skipped over Zach Trotter. How do you explain his disappearance?"

"Here's how I see it," Bree said, pursing her lips judiciously. "Zach comes home drunk for the hundredth time, falls down the stairs, cracks his head open, and bleeds all over the rag rug Annabelle *made by hand* for her foyer. It's the last straw. She kicks him out of the house in the middle of the night and tells him never to darken her doorway again. When asked, she says he left her. She'd rather be pitied as an abandoned wife than reviled as a termagant."

"Okay," I said slowly. "But why did she bury the rug?"

"She didn't want to put it out with the trash, where everyone could see it," Bree said without hesitation. "She was ashamed of her ratbag husband's bloodstains."

"Answer one more question and you win a prize," I said. "If Annabelle's innocent on all counts, why on earth did she tell me she killed Zach?"

"No idea," said Bree. "Maybe she's skipping her meds, too."

Bree had come up with a reassuring number of ifs and maybes, but I was no more convinced by them than I had been by Hayley Calthorp's assertions. The only way to prove our case one way or the other seemed to involve trespass as well as the wanton destruction of private property.

I wondered if it was time to purchase a spade.

■ ■ ■ ■

After a snack and a diaper change, Bess took Bree for a romp in the walled garden. I touched base with Amelia, who assured me that Stanley was eating his cat food with carefree abandon and that all was well at the cottage. I strongly suspected her of supplementing Stanley's diet with delicate slices of salmon and chunks of smoked trout, as she had in the past, but I didn't object. With Bill away, Stanley needed his comfort food.

I could hear Bill easily when I called him. He gave the steam train in Ravenglass a stellar review, but Will and Rob were too busy rock hunting to share their opinions with me. I told him that Bree, Bess, and I had spent the day learning about Old Cowerton's history. I didn't specify the exact period of history, or the nature of the lessons, but I didn't lie.

When Bree left the suite for a swim and another Mariana massage, Bess was content to play with Moo in the playpen. I lit the hearth's gas fire and pulled the blue journal from my shoulder bag. It was time to touch base with Aunt Dimity.

"Dimity?" I said as I settled back in an

armchair. "It's been a strange day."

The curving lines of royal-blue ink appeared instantly on the page, as if Aunt Dimity had been waiting for me to check in.

Good afternoon, Lori. You seem to be having nothing but strange days lately.

"This one was stranger than most," I said.

Did you and Bree go to Dovecote?

"Oh, yes," I said. "We saw the infamous rosebushes and we attended a tea party held in our honor by none other than Minnie Jessop. . . ." I told Aunt Dimity about Susan Jessop, Sunnyside, Minnie's spy ring, and the cronies, and I summarized the Sunnyside Gang's tragic tales concerning Zach Trotter, Ted Fletcher, Jim Salford, William Walker May, and Edwin Craven. "You can forget all about Annabelle murdering one man," I concluded. "At last count, she may have killed *five.*"

Tell me more about the Sunnyside Gang.

"They're nosy old biddies," I said, "but some of my best friends are nosy old biddies. I hope to live long enough to become one myself."

A noble aspiration.

"I expected Minnie Jessop to be a hateful hag with a viper's tongue," I went on, "and in some ways she was. But she also let Bess

211

bang dents in her saucepans. She baked extra goodies for her friends to bring back to the nursing home. She noticed my disappointment over the Melting Moments, and she made sure I had some to take with me. She was even nice to Moo. She wasn't exactly complimentary about Hayley Calthorp, but the only time she was nasty was when she talked about Annabelle."

It's hardly surprising that she would focus her wrath on a woman she believes to be a mass murderess. What does Bree think of the gang's tales?

"She described them as a big bucket of nonsense," I replied.

But you're not quite as ready to dismiss them?

I lifted my gaze to stare into the fire, then lowered it to the journal.

"In Finch," I said, "we love to gossip. But there's a level of gossip to which we will not sink. There's a sort of integrity that governs the tidbits we pass along. It keeps situations from getting out of hand. It keeps people from getting hurt. It's a self-imposed check on gossip's wilder — and crueler — excesses."

A self-imposed check you failed to detect in the Sunnyside Gang.

"They accused Annabelle of the most

heinous crimes," I said. "They told the police to go after her. They tried their best to scare off any man who took a fancy to her. They held a tea party for the sole purpose of undermining our friendship with her. Why would they persecute Annabelle then and now if they didn't truly believe that she was guilty?"

Allow me to remind you that these are the same women who truly believe in the widow's curse.

"They may give lip service to the widow's curse," I said, "but they paint a picture of Annabelle as an upwardly mobile serial killer — a social climber who used murder to get ahead." I shrugged. "Who's to say she isn't?"

Hayley Calthorp's gran, for one. I might also point out that there were no eyewitnesses to any of the deaths attributed to Annabelle.

"The lack of eyewitnesses cuts both ways," I insisted. "No one saw her commit the murders, but no one can swear that she didn't commit them, either. The only thing I know for sure is that four men who knew Annabelle lie dead and buried in St. Leonard's churchyard. Four men, Dimity! That's a high rate of mysterious deaths for one small town, isn't it? It's also possible that Zach Trotter is pushing up rosebushes because of her. Their ghosts may not have chased Annabelle away from Craven Manor, but guilt might have."

Then go there.

"Go where?" I said blankly.

Go to St. Leonard's, of course. If the men were buried there, the church is bound to have records of their funerals. Find out if the dates fall within the parameters set by Minnie and her chums. There must be a local newspaper. Dig into the archives for stories about the men's deaths. The library may hold records of the coroner's inquests. The Old Cowerton constabulary will certainly have case files. You've heard nothing but rumors since you arrived in Old Cowerton, my dear. It's time for you to gather facts.

Having spent part of my youth working among rare books, I was unfazed by the prospect of burrowing through dusty files.

"Research, not rumors," I said thoughtfully. "Seems obvious, now that you've spelled it out. Why didn't I think of it?"

I'm sure you would have.

"Thanks for the vote of confidence," I said. "And thanks for the game plan. I'd rather dig through archives than dig up rosebushes."

A prudent preference, as the former is less likely to get you arrested than the latter.

"I'll go to St. Leonard's tomorrow," I said. "Bree can look after Bess while I tackle —" I broke off at the sound of a gentle knock on the hallway door, then whispered, "Gotta go, Dimity. I'll let you know what I find."

I'm sure you'll find something!

I stashed the journal in my shoulder bag and ran to open the door. Francesco stood in the hallway, clutching a small cream-colored envelope.

"Hello, Francesco," I said. "We spent the day with Minnie Jessop. She and her friends told us about *the others.*"

"I'm so sorry, madam," Francesco said, his brow furrowing. "I hope it did not upset you."

"As a matter of fact, it did," I said, "but I'm sometimes too impressionable for my own good."

"So are we all, madam." He handed the envelope to me. "A message for you, delivered by hand to the front desk not ten minutes ago. Is there anything else I can do for you?"

"Not at the moment," I said. "We'll order dinner as soon as Bree —" I broke off again as I spotted Bree sauntering unhurriedly up the corridor, clad in the hotel's robe and floppy slippers.

"You look relaxed," I commented when

she was within earshot.

"You really must let Mariana work her magic on you before we leave, Lori," she said. "I feel like a bowl of melted ice cream. Hi, Francesco," she went on, stopping beside him. "Did Lori tell you that we know about *the others*?"

"She did, madam," he replied mournfully. "I hope Mrs. Jessop's stories did not disturb you."

"Do I look disturbed?" Bree asked with a drowsy titter.

"Not at all," he said, smiling down at her. He assured us that dinner would be served at our convenience, bowed to each of us, and strode down the corridor toward the lobby.

Bree followed me into the sitting room, gazing curiously at the envelope.

"Fan mail?" she asked, sprawling lazily on the sofa.

"I'll let you know," I replied. I opened the envelope and withdrew a handwritten note.

"If it's an invitation to another Sunnyside tea party, I'm in," Bree said languidly. "Minnie's plum cake was superb."

"It's an invitation," I said, "but it isn't from Minnie Jessop."

I passed the note to Bree and waited for her reaction.

"Good grief," she said, sitting bolt upright. "We've been summoned to Craven Manor!"

SEVENTEEN

Our "summons" was, in fact, a politely worded invitation to brunch written on deckle-edged notepaper by a woman named Penelope Moorecroft. I dialed the phone number scrawled at the bottom of the page, hoping to find out who Penelope Moorecroft was, but the voice that accepted our RSVP was decidedly male, formal, and reticent. I ended the call none the wiser.

"Butler, I think," I said in response to Bree's inquiring look. "A tight-lipped successor to William Walker May."

"Penelope Moorecroft must be the current lady of the manor," she said. "A cook or a poor relation wouldn't have the clout to invite us to brunch. Why do you suppose she wants to meet us?"

"I don't know," I said, "but if she lays any more corpses at Annabelle's feet, I'll need a sedative."

I filed Aunt Dimity's proposed research

project under "later" and got on with our evening routine, but as I read *Wuthering Heights* aloud to Bess after dinner, I couldn't help wondering if Edwin Craven roamed the halls at Craven Manor in the same way that Heathcliff's unquiet spirit roamed the moors.

I didn't have to consult our map or rely on Francesco for directions to Craven Manor. The estate could be seen for miles. A pair of wrought-iron gates blocking the drive swung open after a pair of cameras scanned the Range Rover, and we entered a green, sloping landscape dotted with extremely woolly sheep. Bess mooed at them enthusiastically.

"Cotswold Lions," I said.

"Pardon?" said Bree.

"Cotswold Lions," I repeated, waving a hand at the flock. "It's a rare breed of sheep. Their wool made the Cotswolds rich until the middle of the eighteenth century, when the local wool industry began to go belly-up. They're why so many small towns in the Cotswolds have such magnificent churches. The so-called wool churches were built by fabulously wealthy landowners whose fortunes were based almost entirely on Cotswold Lions."

"They're adorable," said Bree. "I prefer rich people who spend their money on preserving rare breeds to those who fritter it away on handbags, high heels, and hairdos. If our mystery hostess is the lady of the manor, I already have a high opinion of her."

Craven Manor reminded me of my father-in-law's home, Fairworth House. Both were solid, respectable Georgian mansions, and though Craven Manor was quite a bit larger than Fairworth, it was made from the same golden Cotswold stone and possessed the same aura of timeless tranquillity.

Bluebell Cottage, I thought, would fit easily in one wing of the manor. It struck me that Annabelle would have needed a very good reason to leave such a splendid and spacious estate for a tiny cottage overlooking a village green.

The wide flight of stone steps leading to the front door had been retrofitted with a wooden ramp, possibly to accommodate a wheelchair. As I wheeled the all-terrain pram up the ramp, I wondered if Annabelle had installed it for her ailing husband.

We were ushered into the entrance hall by a butler whose voice I recognized from the RSVP call. He was less haughty in person, though no more forthcoming.

"Mrs. Moorecroft will be with you

shortly," he informed us. "May I take your coats?"

As Bree and I doffed our jackets, I allowed my gaze to travel from the entrance hall's sweeping marble staircase to its oversized chandelier. It was all too easy to picture Mabel's cousin Florence skidding to a halt on the marble floor while Annabelle gazed down from the landing. When I forced myself to glance at the spot where Edwin's lifeless body would have lain, I felt the same queasy feeling I'd felt when I'd seen Sunnyside's foyer.

A door at the back of the hall opened and a tall, white-haired woman with piercing blue eyes strode toward us. She wore an elegant woven wool tunic over black leggings and black leather ankle boots. Her wrists were adorned with chunky gold bracelets that set off her long, slender fingers, and her short hair had been expertly styled to flatter her high cheekbones and her aquiline nose.

"I guess some people can afford nice clothes *and* rare sheep," Bree murmured.

"Forgive me for keeping you waiting," the woman said, coming to a halt before us. "I was delayed by a crisis in the kitchen. What an enchanting child!" she exclaimed, bending to peer at Bess. "Which one of you is her mother?"

"That would be me," I said. "I'm Lori Shepherd and she's Bess Willis."

"And I'm Bree Pym," said Bree.

"Of course you are," said the woman, straightening. "I'm Penelope Moorecroft, but I do hope you'll call me Penny. Thank you so much for coming."

"Thank you for inviting us," said Bree. "We were admiring your sheep."

"Were you?" said Penny. "They're film stars, as it happens. Directors borrow the flock to add verisimilitude to period pieces. We have a handsome herd of Friesians as well, but they're in the top pasture today." She touched a finger to her lips, then said, "I'm afraid we may be some time over brunch. I wonder if Bess might be happier in the nursery? It has every toy she could possibly desire, a fully stocked pantry, and best of all, it has Nanny Sutton." She turned to extend an arm to a young woman who trotted down the grand staircase to join us.

Nanny Sutton bore no resemblance whatsoever to the mental image I'd formed of her. Her hair was long, dark, and curly instead of short, straight, and gray, and instead of a starched uniform, she wore a cheerful red cotton pullover, blue jeans, and sneakers. I doubted that she was more than a year or two past her twenties, but she exuded an air of competent good humor I wished I could emulate. When Bess mooed at her, she mooed back.

"You work for the White Hart, don't you?" I asked her.

"I'm a freelance nanny," she explained. "The White Hart is only one of my clients."

"Nanny Sutton has a client list Mary Poppins would envy," Penny said. "She has reams of qualifications and nothing but the most glowing recommendations. Your daughter would be in the safest of safe hands."

"It's a tempting offer," I said to the nanny, "but I'd like to see how you and Bess get along before I turn her over to you."

"If Bess were my daughter, I'd do the same thing," said Nanny Sutton. "May I?"

She reached tentatively for the pram's handles and I let her take them.

"Lovely," said Penny. "Shall we join the others?"

I was beginning to twitch every time someone uttered the phrase "the others," but I joined the parade as Bree, Nanny Sutton, and Bess followed our hostess down a central corridor that led to a capacious conservatory attached to the rear of the house. William Walker May could have grown a thousand Amazon lilies in it, but I suspected that his little greenhouse had been demolished after his death as a mark of respect and, perhaps, to erase a troubling memory. When I looked through the glass walls, I saw no sign of it.

There were no flowers in the conservatory. Instead, it held a scattering of feathery ferns and abstract wooden sculptures. I wasn't a huge fan of abstract art, but the sculptures' curving forms appealed to me. They seemed as organic as the ferns.

A wave of déjà vu crashed into me when I saw four white-haired women seated at a round glass-topped table in the center of the conservatory. Though the setting was more sophisticated than Minnie Jessop's back garden, the women regarded us with the same bright-eyed interest as the cronies.

Champagne bottles protruded from a Regency wine cooler beside the round table, and an oblong table to our left held an array of chafing dishes, domed platters, cut-glass pitchers, and silver carafes, but none of the women had filled a glass or a plate. I assumed that Penny's friends were better fed than Minnie's. They were certainly better dressed, though none was as well dressed as Penny.

"I think Bess might like to stretch her legs

in the garden," Nanny Sutton suggested, as Bess strained against the pram's harness. "You'll be able to see us through the glass, and if she misses her mum, I'll bring her straight back to you."

"Her diapers are in the blue bag," I told her, "and her toys are in the yellow one. She's had her midmorning snack, but she'll need to eat again around eleven. You'll find her lunch in the insulated bag."

"May I take her upstairs to the nursery if your brunch runs long?" Nanny Sutton asked. "Penny designed it for her grand-children and her great-grandchildren. I can guarantee that she didn't decorate it with lead paint, rusty nails, and poisonous plants."

I laughed but said, "Let's see how it goes in the garden."

Nanny Sutton gave me a thumbs-up, then wheeled the pram through a pair of French doors that opened out onto a formal knot garden.

"Excellent!" Penny exclaimed. "One of our number is running late, but she urged us to carry on without her. Introductions first, then we'll dig in. Lori Shepherd and Bree Pym, please allow me to present" — she pointed at each woman in turn — "Lorna Small, Alice Johnson, Debbie Lacey, and Gladys Miller."

The women bobbed their heads at us amiably, then rose to their feet to help themselves to food and drink. Penny motioned for us to join them, then bustled about, making mimosas and urging everyone to have more of everything. After directing Bree and me to chairs facing the knot garden, she slid a miniscule portion of caviar onto her plate and sat across from us, with Gladys Miller on her left and an empty chair on her right.

"You must be dying to know why you're here," she said to us.

"My guess," Bree said shrewdly, "is that it has something to do with a tea party we attended yesterday."

"Aren't you clever!" Penny said, smiling sweetly at Bree. "You're absolutely correct as well. When my friends and I heard that Mrs. Jessop had imposed herself upon you, we simply had to do *something* to counteract her libelous claims."

Bree and I didn't bother to ask how news of a tea party in the terraces had reached Craven Manor. It was clear that Old Cowerton's grapevine was even more far-reaching than Finch's.

"We were worried that you'd believe Minnie," said Lorna Small.

"We couldn't stand idly by while she ruined a good woman's reputation," said Alice Johnson.

"We'd blame ourselves if you left Old Cowerton thinking ill of Annabelle," said Debbie Lacey.

"Hence, our little gathering," said Penny. She turned to Gladys Miller. "Would it be unfair of me to ask you to go first, darling? You've barely nibbled your kippers."

"My kippers will keep." Gladys wet her lips with a sip of mimosa, then gazed levelly across the table at Bree and me. "I'm Bob Nash's sister," she said, "and I can tell you exactly how Ted Fletcher died."

EIGHTEEN

"You're the jilted fiancée!" Bree blurted, goggling at Gladys. "Ted Fletcher dumped you when he fell for Annabelle Trotter!"

"*Bree,*" I muttered, mortified by her bluntness.

I blushed on her behalf as the other women clucked their tongues, rolled their eyes, and tossed their heads indignantly. Penny's next comment seemed to indicate, however, that they were upset with someone other than my tactless companion.

"Item one on the long list of lies you've been told," she said. "We've heard them all before, and I'm pleased to say that Gladys can set the record straight on several of them." She held up an index finger. "First, the jilting."

"Ted Fletcher couldn't have jilted me," Gladys said, smiling wryly, "because we were never engaged. My brother Bob wanted me to marry his best friend — he had his heart set on it — but Ted and I were never anything but good pals. We went to the same school and we both worked at the Old Cowerton Dairy, but there was nothing remotely romantic about our relationship. I was much closer to Annabelle than I was to Ted."

"So Annabelle wasn't your rival," Bree said, sounding intrigued. "She was your friend."

"She was my very dear friend," said Gladys, "and she was no more in love with Ted than I was. She tried her best to keep him at arm's length, but she couldn't keep him from falling in love with her."

"She was a very pretty girl," Penny said, "and she'd been treated abominably by her detestable husband. She brought out the white knight in Ted."

"He was always showing up on her door-step," said Gladys. "He wouldn't let her replace a lightbulb without his help. He went into transports about her whenever our paths crossed at the dairy. I told him it was no good, but the heart wants what the heart wants."

"Did you work at the dairy at the same time as Mildred Greenham?" Bree asked.

"Yes," said Gladys. "Mildred worked in the front office, I worked in the cheese-making kitchens, and Annabelle and I had our picnic lunches on a hillock above the south pasture."

"*Your* picnic lunches?" I said sharply.

"I thought that would get your attention," Penny said with a knowing nod. "As I said, we've heard it all before. Set the record straight about the picnic hamper, will you, Gladys?"

"With pleasure," said Gladys. She took another sip from her glass before continuing, "When Annabelle had a moment to spare from her own work, she'd pack a hamper and bring it along to the dairy around lunchtime." She smiled reminiscently. "It wasn't a gourmet feast, like Penny's brunch. We had fish paste sandwiches and a few apples more often than not, but we pretended the hamper was from Fortnum's and enjoyed every bite."

"Were you and Annabelle enjoying fish paste sandwiches on the day Ted Fletcher died?" I asked, although the answer seemed inevitable.

"We were," said Gladys. "With the notable exception of Mildred Greenham, any fool will tell you that the view from our hillock was a good deal better than the view from the front office." She bowed her head. "I wish it hadn't been. I'd give anything to

230

forget what I saw that day. We screamed for help when we saw Ted stumble and fall into the muck, but we were too far away to make ourselves heard. We could do nothing but stand there and watch as he . . . as he . . . ." Her voice trailed off, as if she couldn't bear to describe the nightmarish scene she'd witnessed.

"There, there, Gladys," Penny said, putting a comforting arm around her friend. "You've been very brave. You needn't upset yourself further. We'll let Debbie take it from here. Debbie?"

Debbie Lacey was short and plump and made of sterner stuff than I. She'd continued to ply her knife and fork with undisguised gusto throughout Gladys's harrowing description of Ted Fletcher's gruesome death, stopping only when Penny called on her to say her piece. It was with the greatest reluctance that she laid her utensils aside and addressed Bree and me.

"Before I got married," she said, "I worked as a kitchen maid here at the manor. One of my chores was to collect wild mushrooms. Cook knew that Mr. Craven was fond of wild mushrooms, and he liked to use fresh ones in his dishes, so he taught me which ones were safe to eat and where I was likely to find them. I was out hunting for mushrooms on the morning Jim Salford drowned."

"Tell them *where* you were, darling," Penny coaxed, as though she were speaking to a dim-witted child.

"I was right across the river from Jim and Annabelle," said Debbie. "I'd just found a lovely patch of chanterelles when I heard them talking. Jim was showing off for Annabelle, bragging about his catches, and not paying a lick of attention to where he was standing. You have to be careful in the spring," she informed us in a cautionary aside, "because the rushing water can undercut the bank."

"Which is precisely what happened," Penny interjected.

Debbie nodded. "Jim went too near the edge of the bank and it gave way under him. Annabelle only just saved herself by grabbing onto a tree, but Jim went straight into the river. He was swept away before we could do anything about it." She shrugged. "Jim was a strong swimmer, but once the current took him, he didn't stand a chance."

"And *after* he was swept away?" Penny prompted. "Tell them what you did then."

"Annabelle looked too shaken up to walk out of the woods on her own," said Debbie, "so I hollered at her to sit tight while I hightailed it back to the big house to ring the police. I told them where to find her, and they brought her here. I wrapped her in a blanket and Cook gave her a cup of tea because she was all shivery. I reckon she was in shock."

"What about Jim?" Bree asked.

"They found his body three days later, caught up in some rocks downstream," Debbie replied, adding sadly, "They never did find his fishing rod."

I restrained an insane urge to laugh at her sorrow for such a trivial loss.

"Well done, darling," said Penny. "Now tell them about William Walker."

Bree turned to Debbie and asked, "Were you still working here when William Walker May died?"

"Course I was," said Debbie. "I didn't get married until a year later, not that I wanted to wait, but my husband had to finish his national service before we could even think of —"

"William Walker?" Penny interrupted hopefully.

"Right," said Debbie, regaining her focus. "People — *ignorant* people — can say what they like about Annabelle, but I know for a fact that she didn't kill William Walker. I could see his little greenhouse through the kitchen windows. Annabelle never went near it unless he went with her."

"William Walker didn't win bags of blue ribbons at the flower show by being careless," Penny said. "Flower shows are rather cutthroat affairs in Old Cowerton."

"It's the same in our village," said Bree.

"Then you'll understand why William Walker kept a close watch over his greenhouse," said Penny.

"William Walker's Amazon lilies were his pride and joy," said Debbie. "He kept them under lock and key — and he had the only key. He wouldn't let anyone, not even Mr. Craven, set foot in his greenhouse without him. Besides, Annabelle was hopeless with machinery."

"She did all of her sewing by hand," said Gladys, "because sewing machines made her nervous."

"Anyone who says she tampered with the heater in William Walker's greenhouse is a liar," Debbie concluded, not bothering to mince words. "Even if she somehow managed to make a copy of the key *and* to slip past the kitchen windows without me or Cook noticing, she wouldn't have had the know-how to nobble the heater."

"There you are," said Penny. "Two reliable witnesses who testified to both the police and the coroner that the deaths of Ted Fletcher, Jim Salford, and William Walker May, while tragic, were accidental."

"My boss and three of my coworkers — who are sadly no longer with us — saw Ted fall into the slurry pit," said Gladys. "All six of us testified that he died in a workplace accident."

"A geologist at Jim's inquest blamed his drowning on erosion," said Debbie. "And the company that manufactured the greenhouse heater admitted that it was faulty."

"We don't expect you to take our word for it," said Penny. "I have a complete file on each case — newspaper clippings, police reports, postmortem documents, church records, inquest transcripts . . ." She paused to take a breath, then continued, "If Gladys and Debbie haven't convinced you that Annabelle is entirely innocent of the absurd accusations leveled against her by certain members of our community, I'll be happy to show you the files."

Bree and I stared at her curiously.

"Why do you have files on —" I began, but I was cut off midsentence by the late entrance of the last of Penny's guests.

"Sorry!" Susan Jessop called as she hurried to take her place next to our hostess. "I thought my committee meeting would never end!"

"You couldn't have arrived at a better time, darling," said Penny, kissing Susan on both cheeks. "We were about to tell Lori and Bree why your mother is the least reliable witness on God's green earth."

NINETEEN

"Hello again," Susan Jessop said, waving to us across the glass-topped table.

"Hi," Bree and I chorused reflexively. Bree seemed to be as taken aback as I was to see Susan at a gathering of her mother's harshest critics.

"If you don't mind," said Susan, "I'll snag a little something from the buffet before we continue. I didn't have time to eat breakfast at home, and the doughnuts at the meeting were gone before I got there."

"Snag away," I told her. "We're not going anywhere."

"Unlike the doughnuts," Susan said drily.

While Bree and the other women served themselves second helpings of kippers, eggs Benedict, smoked salmon kedgeree, strawberry crepes, chocolate pancakes, and crème fraîche–daubed caviar, I strolled across the conservatory to look through a glass wall at the knot garden. Bess and Nanny Sutton ared to be playing a game not unlike Bad Bear among the meticulously immed box hedges. If my daughter was traumatized by my absence, she hid it well. Her dribbly grin persuaded me that she was in very good hands indeed.

"What on earth is *Susan* doing here?" Bree whispered, crossing to stand beside me. "Is she some kind of mole — a double agent planted in Sunnyside to spy on her own mother?"

"Could be," I whispered back. "Why don't you ask her?"

"I will," said Bree.

She was as good as her word. When everyone was seated, she folded her arms and asked without preamble, "What are you doing here, Susan?"

"I'm here for the same reason as Penny, Gladys, Debbie, Lorna, and Alice," Susan replied. "I couldn't let my mother poison your friendship with Annabelle Craven." She held up her hand. "Don't misunderstand me. I love and admire my mother. She raised six of us in that little house. She saw to it that we had a good education and she taught us the value of hard work. No one could have done more for us." Susan dropped her hand and grimaced apologetically. "But she's mistaken about Annabelle.

238

Always has been, always will be."

"Mistaken?" I repeated irately. "Your mother has spent half her life tormenting Annabelle."

"More than half her life, actually," Susan said without rancor. "It began on the night Zach Trotter disappeared." She looked at the two women who hadn't yet spoken in Annabelle's defense. "Alice? Lorna? If you'll walk us through what really happened that night?"

Alice Johnson and Lorna Small had already set aside their knives and forks, as though they'd expected Susan to call upon them. When she did, they straightened their shoulders and lifted their chins, much as Mabel Parson had done when speaking of Edwin Craven at Minnie's tea party. Annabelle's friends, like her enemies, seemed to take their storytelling responsibilities very seriously.

"When I was a young married lady," Alice began, "I lived on Parkview Terrace in the terraces. Parkview Terrace is one street over from Bellevue Terrace, where the Trotters and the Jessops lived."

"I lived next door to Alice," said Lorna. "The thing you have to understand is that our back bedrooms overlooked Bellevue Terrace."

"My back bedroom overlooked Dovecote, where the Trotters lived," Alice clarified. "I couldn't see their back garden from my window, but I could see their front door. I could hear it, too, every time Zach slammed it."

"We liked Annabelle," said Lorna, "but we couldn't stand her husband."

"No one in the neighborhood could stand him," said Alice.

"Zach Trotter would pinch the grass from your garden if you didn't keep an eye on him," Lorna said, making no effort to conceal her contempt. "And he was always coming home drunk."

"Sometimes he'd sing silly songs and sometimes he'd knock over rubbish bins and he nearly always slammed the door," said Alice. "He made such a racket that my husband and I had to move from our back bedroom to our front bedroom, just to get a night's rest."

"My husband and I had to do the same thing," Lorna chimed in.

"I had a touch of bronchitis one summer," Alice said, placing a hand on her chest. "I didn't want to keep my husband up half the night with my coughing, so I moved into the back bedroom. He was the breadwinner, you see, and he needed his eight hours."

"With bronchitis, you always get worse before you get better," Lorna said knowledgeably. "When Alice got really bad, I stayed at her place to look after her. I slept on a camp bed in her room, so she wouldn't be on her own."

I tried to imagine a world in which Bill would allow a neighbor to tend to me during a serious illness instead of caring for me himself, but I couldn't manage it. I felt incredibly lucky to have a husband who could afford to take time off from work when his family needed him.

"I was sitting up with Alice when Zach came home that night," Lorna continued, and no one had to ask which night "that night" was. "He wasn't making a racket for once, but I could hear him fumbling with his key. It must have been an hour later when I heard Dovecote's door open again. Alice was dozing, so I got up to look through the window."

"When Lorna got up, I woke up," said Alice, "and I went to look, too."

I felt a rush of affection for Alice. Like my neighbors in Finch, she wouldn't allow ill health to rob her of a chance to snoop.

"We watched from the window as Zach stepped outside," Lorna said.

"Did he have a bandage on his head?"

241

Bree asked, thinking no doubt of the allegedly bloodstained rag rug.

"He didn't have a bandage on any part of him that we could see," said Lorna.

"And we could see him plain as day," Alice put in, "because of the light coming through a gap in the curtains in Annabelle's bay window."

"He stood on the doorstep for a bit," said Lorna, "as if he couldn't decide what to do next. Then he stuck his hands in his pockets and walked down Bellevue Terrace."

"He slipped out of Old Cowerton like a thief in the night," said Alice. "We never saw him again."

"Good riddance to bad rubbish," Lorna stated firmly.

"We saw Zach walk away from Dovecote *on his own two feet,*" Alice stressed. "We saw him abandon Annabelle without a backward glance, and so we told the nice young constable when he came round to question us."

"If Minnie hadn't been spying on Annabelle in the back garden, she might have seen Zach leave through the front door," said Lorna.

"I'm sure Minnie saw Annabelle bury something in the back garden," said Alice, "but it wasn't Zach's corpse because Zach wasn't dead."

"Dead men don't walk," Lorna said.

"We told Minnie she was mistaken," said Alice, "but once she got a notion into her head, she wouldn't let go of it."

"Why let the truth get in the way of a good story?" Penny asked sardonically.

"I'd have sued her for defamation," said Lorna, "but Annabelle was too busy making ends meet to worry about nasty gossip."

"Annabelle knew who her friends were," Gladys piped up, "and she didn't count Minnie Jessop and her crowd among them. Sorry, Susan," she added with a penitant glance at Minnie's daughter.

Susan, who'd been making up for her missed breakfast, didn't appear to be offended. To the contrary, she dismissed Gladys's apology with a nonchalant shrug.

"I'm familiar with my mother's shortcomings as well as her admirable qualities," she said. "I also understand why she still feels compelled to prove her case against Annabelle."

"Maybe you should explain it," said Bree, "because I still don't get it."

"I'm a teacher," Susan responded good-naturedly. "I never turn down an invitation to explain things." She washed down a mouthful of crepe with a swig of coffee, gave a satisfied sigh, and settled back in her chair. "Zach's disappearance was one of the most momentous events in my mother's life — and one of the most frustrating. She honestly believed that Annabelle had murdered him, and she was outraged when the police refused to take her eyewitness account seriously. She felt as if she'd been shunted aside and ignored because the police saw her as a working-class yob who couldn't be trusted to tell the truth. Her outrage made her cling to her accusation even after Alice and Lorna proved it was false."

"She wasn't the only one to make a false accusation," Bree pointed out. "Her friends made a few of their own, and she went along with them."

"My mother was already convinced that Annabelle was capable of murder," said Susan. "She had no trouble believing her friends when they added a few more alleged victims to the body count."

"But why did her friends feel the need to add to the body count?" Bree asked. "I can just about understand why Minnie thought what she thought about Annabelle, but I don't understand her friends. They didn't actually *see* Annabelle kill *anyone.* Why were they so willing to think the worst of her?"

"Jealousy," Gladys replied. "Even when we were at school together, they were jealous of Annabelle. They were as plain as pugs and as dull as cold porridge. She was as pretty as a princess and as bright as a new penny." She smiled. "Even her name was prettier than theirs."

"They couldn't have been jealous of Annabelle after she married Zach," I said, shaking my head. "He wasn't what I'd call a great catch."

"I imagine her ill-judged marriage allowed them to feel superior to her for a while," Penny said reflectively. "Once Zach disappeared, though, and a string of attractive chaps began to pursue her, their sense of inferiority must have reasserted itself."

"And like a pack of jackals, they decided to bring her down," said Gladys.

Susan Jessop raised an eyebrow. "If you're fair, you'll admit that an alarming number of Annabelle's suitors died prematurely."

"True enough," Gladys agreed. "But they also died accidentally."

"Except for Zach," I said. "He walked off into the night and vanished without a trace. We don't know what happened to him."

"In point of fact, we do," said Penny, raising a slender finger to catch my attention. "My late brother discovered where Zach

went and what he did after he left Old Cowerton."

"Was your brother a policeman?" I asked.

"No," said Penny. "He was Annabelle's
second husband. You may have heard of
him. His name was Edwin Craven."

Bree dropped her fork.

"Y-you're Annabelle's *sister-in-law?*" I
stammered, thunderstruck.

"I am," said Penny, smiling delightedly at
our reactions. "I'm so pleased no one tipped
you off. I'm rather fond of surprises."

"We're surprised," Bree acknowledged.
Ignoring her fallen fork, she gazed per-
plexedly at Penny, then asked, "Is it true
that William Walker introduced Annabelle
to your brother?"

"Certainly not," said Penny. "William
Walker would have thought it highly im-
proper to introduce a mere seamstress to
his employer. Edwin and Annabelle met
quite by chance. He walked in on her while
she was mending a torn tapestry in the
music room. A look passed between them
and that was that."

There was a touch of frost in Bree's manner when she asked, "How did you feel
about your brother marrying a *mere seamstress?*"

"I never regarded Annabelle as a mere

seamstress," Penny responded easily. "I used the phrase simply to illustrate William Walker's prejudices. I knew from the moment I met Annabelle that she was Edwin's ideal mate. They had the same sense of humor and the same deep appreciation of beauty." Penny chuckled. "They even shared a fondness for wild mushrooms! If ever a match was meant to be, it was theirs. My only regret was that they had to postpone their wedding until they could ascertain whether Annabelle's marriage to Zach was still valid."

"Which is why your brother set out to discover what happened to Zach," I said, nodding.

"He was also determined to refute the vile accusations made against his intended by Minnie and her chatty chums," said Penny. "The files I mentioned were his."

"It sounds as though Annabelle brought out the white knight in your brother," I said, smiling.

"Any decent man familiar with the trials Annabelle endured throughout her first marriage would feel protective of her," said Penny. "Fortunately, Edwin had the means to track Zach's movements. It took him the better part of three years to do it, but he eventually succeeded in retracing Zach's steps from a cargo ship in Liverpool to a rather uncouth drinking establishment in Adelaide."

"So Zach the drunk ended up in Australia," Bree said. "I can't say I'm surprised."

"Do I detect a Kiwi prejudice?" Penny asked, her eyes twinkling.

I laughed and Bree had the grace to blush.

"By the time my brother caught up with him," Penny continued, "Zach had nearly drunk himself to death. Edwin had no trouble persuading him to go through with a long-distance divorce."

"We couldn't have been happier for Annabelle," said Gladys. "She was finally free to marry the man she was meant to marry."

"She would have been free in any case," said Susan. "Seven years had passed. If Edwin hadn't found Zach, Annabelle could have applied for a legal declaration of death."

"If I'd been Edwin," said Bree, "I would have nailed the divorce papers to Minnie's door."

"Believe me, he wanted to," said Penny, "but Annabelle wouldn't let him. She honestly didn't care about what people like Minnie thought of her. She'd been through so much already — she was eager to put it all behind her and to begin again with a man who was truly worthy of her."

"She didn't even care when they accused her of killing your brother?" Bree asked.

"Not even then," Penny said, losing some of her twinkle. "I would gladly have nailed their mouths shut, darling, but it wouldn't have done any good. They would have brushed aside my eyewitness account as easily as they brushed aside Gladys's."

"Sorry?" said Bree, frowning. "Are you saying that you saw —"

"Oh, yes," Penny interrupted quietly. "I was staying at Craven Manor on the night my brother died."

TWENTY

I could almost feel a wave of sympathy wash over Penny. She blinked rapidly for a moment, then dashed a tear from her eye and laughed, as if to reassure her audience that she was quite all right, thank you. When she spoke again, her voice was as strong and as carefree as it had been before she'd made her startling admission.

"Edwin and I had no other siblings," she said. "Because I was almost ten years his junior, we never quarreled over playthings or competed for our parents' affection. We quite liked each other when we were young and our mutual regard didn't wane as we grew older. We led separate lives for a long time, but we kept in touch with letters, phone calls, holiday visits, and, during our later years, e-mails."

"I wish I were as close with my brother as you were with Edwin," said Gladys, "but once Bob began blaming Annabelle for

Ted's death, I couldn't be in the same room with him without giving him a piece of my mind."

"Bob's no Edwin," said Lorna.

"Hardly anyone is," Penny said with a melancholy smile. "After I lost my husband, Craven Manor became my second home. I had the great good fortune to see my brother happy in his marriage to Annabelle and the great misfortune to see Alzheimer's claim him. It's quite the most dreadful thing I've ever witnessed. Edwin didn't sink peacefully into a fluffy cosmic duvet of forgetfulness. He experienced bizarre hallucinations, paranoia, desperate confusion, and uncontrollable outbursts of rage. He couldn't remember how to dress or to feed himself. Eventually, he lost control of his bodily functions."

She pulled a fresh bottle of champagne from the wine cooler, topped up her mimosa, and took a long sip. I wished I had something stronger to offer her.

"Edwin's illness was an ever-deepening nightmare," she went on. "Annabelle coped for as long as she could, but in the end she had to face the fact that she simply wasn't strong enough to change a grown man's nappies."

Bree winced.

Observing her pained expression, Penny drawled, "The indignities of old age, my dear, are legion."

When I thought of Minnie's dentures, Mildred's hair net, Mabel's hearing aids, Myrtle's hunched back, and the three-pronged metal canes that had startled Bess, I couldn't help but agree with Penny. *Old age,* I reminded myself, *is not for the faint-hearted.*

"Annabelle put Edwin into the very best nursing home she could find within driving distance of Craven Manor," said Penny.

"Cloverhill," said Debbie, nodding.

"The finest nursing home in the county," said Lorna.

"One of the finest in the country," said Alice.

"Cloverhill is a superlative facility," Penny agreed. "Annabelle chose it not only because it was nearby but because its physicians were conversant with cutting-edge treatments for Alzheimer's patients." She shook her head. "Edwin responded to none of them. Annabelle visited him every day, even though he didn't know who she was, except that, sometimes, he did. Perhaps the cruelest aspect of that cruel disease is that it allows its victims to surface from time to time, regardless of treatments. Once in a great while Edwin would say something that made Annabelle believe he was *in there* somewhere, waiting for her to rescue him."

"Is that why she brought him home?" Bree asked hesitantly. "Was it something he said?"

"He looked directly into her eyes and he said her name." Penny sighed. "It was enough to make her decide to bring him back to the manor. A foolish decision, perhaps, but I understood it. The last thing Alzheimer's destroys is hope, but Annabelle clung to the hope that familiar surroundings would bring him back to her."

Gladys wiped her eyes surreptitiously with a napkin, and Alice sniffed.

"Annabelle hired a nurse to help with the heavy lifting and to sit with him through the night," said Penny. "And I came to Craven Manor with the intention of staying for as long as she needed me."

The blanket of sorrow that had settled over the conservatory was lifted by Nanny Sutton, who chose that moment to wheel the pram through the French doors while allowing Bess to cling to her finger and toddle alongside her.

"The wind's come up," she announced. "I thought it might be best to beat a retreat to the nursery."

"Go ahead," I told her. "I know she'll be fine."

My new acquaintances stirred themselves to say sweet things about my daughter, but Bess was too enchanted by her new playmate to pay attention to them. She allowed me to give her a hug and a kiss before demanding to be released, then made a slow and unsteady exit with Nanny Sutton.

"Your little girl is a breath of fresh air," Penny said. "It's good to be reminded of beginnings when we're speaking of endings." She handed the champagne bottle to Susan and told her to pass it around. "Not far to go now, but I think we could all do with another drop of bubbly to see us through."

Since I was driving, I let the bottle pass me by, but no one else followed my example. By the time the bottle found its way back to the wine cooler, there wasn't a drop of bubbly left in it.

"Where was I before our charming and most welcome interruption?" Penny asked. "Ah, yes, I remember." She took a deep breath and continued briskly, "On the night Edwin died, I stopped by Annabelle's bedroom for a chat. I was leaving her room when I saw Edwin in his nightshirt, shuffling toward the staircase. I shouted for him

254

to stop, but he took no notice. He fell before I could reach him. I knew without looking that he was dead. No one could have survived such a fall, least of all a frail old man."

Debbie took a healthy swig of champagne and the others followed suit.

"Annabelle ran up beside me and froze," said Penny. "She was paralyzed with horror, but I was incensed. I marched straight into Edwin's bedroom and found the hired nurse asleep in her chair."

"That must be why Mabel Parson's cousin Florence didn't see you at the top of the stairs," Bree interjected. "By the time she reached the front hall, you were in Edwin's room."

"By the time Florence reached the front hall," Penny said crisply, "I was shaking the nurse until her teeth rattled. At least, it sounded like teeth rattling. What I actually heard was the sound of Edwin's sleeping tablets falling on the floor. The wicked woman had *pocketed* them!"

"Aha," Bree breathed, as another false accusation was soundly quashed.

"An inquiry revealed that she'd been stealing medication from her patients for years and selling it online to feather her own nest," said Penny. "She wasn't merely careless; she was criminal. I'm pleased to say that she was struck off the nurses' register and sentenced to an impressively long prison term for negligent homicide and a host of other charges."

I found the news of the nurse's imprisonment grimly satisfying, but Bree was determined to tie up yet another loose end.

"Mabel told us that her cousin thought she saw a look of relief cross Annabelle's face," she said. "Did you see it, too?"

"If Annabelle was relieved," Penny said impatiently, "it was because a merciful God had finally taken her husband to a better place, though in my humble opinion, a *truly* merciful God would have taken him sooner. Having seen her suffering as well as Edwin's, I was deeply relieved to know that my husband had dropped dead of a heart attack!"

"I'd feel the same way," said Bree, unabashed. "Death isn't the worst thing that can happen to someone we love."

"Far from it." Penny collected herself, then went on. "I hoped that Annabelle would stay on at Craven Manor, but she simply couldn't. Edwin's prolonged illness and his violent death had tainted the memories of the happier times they'd shared here. I feared that in years to come she might regret her decision, so I purchased the manor from her to hold it in trust, as it were, should she ever choose to return. I live here, but it's also my workplace. I have a studio in the east wing and I use the conservatory as a gallery. The natural light makes it a perfect showplace for my sculptures."

"So the sculptures are yours," I said, swiveling in my chair to survey the abstract wooden figures. "They're beautiful."

"Thank you," said Penny. "One of the reasons Annabelle and I got along so well is that we're both artists — she with her needle, I with my chisel."

"She's still an artist," I said. "Her baby quilts are exquisite."

"They always were," said Penny.

"I hope you won't mind my asking," I said, "but if you and Annabelle get along so well, why haven't you visited her in Finch?"

"She hasn't invited me," Penny replied. "I suspect it's because I'm woven inextricably into her painful memories." She peered inquiringly at me. "I confess to no little curiosity about her new home. What's it like?"

"She lives in a cottage beside our village green," I said. "Her cottage is comfortable, but it's quite a bit smaller than Craven Manor."

"It's smaller than your conservatory," Bree put in.

Penny nodded. "That would explain why she took so little with her — a few sticks of furniture, her sewing things, her collection of fabrics, and a Victorian quilt frame Edwin gave her as a birthday gift."

"We've seen the quilt frame," I said. "Annabelle set it up in our village hall less than a week ago. We used it for a quilting bee." I took a bracing slurp of unadulterated orange juice before continuing, "You may find it hard to believe, but I was sitting across from Annabelle at the quilt frame when she told me she killed Zach."

Five pairs of eyes stared at me and two mouths fell open, but no one spoke until Penny found her voice.

"I beg your pardon?" she said, frowning slightly.

"She came right out with it," I said. "She told me she hit him on the head with a poker after she pushed him down the stairs. Then she rolled him up in a rug, dragged him into her back garden, and buried him in the trench she'd dug for her rosebushes. She was very convincing — so convincing, in fact, that Bree and I came to Old Cowerton for the sole purpose of finding out if by some remote possibility she might have told me the truth."

"If you've learned nothing else today," said Susan, "I hope you've learned that Annabelle didn't murder Zach."

"I don't believe that Annabelle murdered anyone," I said, "but she seems to think she did. Can any of you explain why she would confess to killing Zach?"

"Not going dotty, is she?" asked Debbie.

"I don't think so," I said.

"Nor do I," said Bree. "She's just as sharp now as she was when she moved to Finch."

"I suppose she could have been having a little fun with you," Gladys said hesitantly. "She's always had a playful streak."

"Would you describe yourself as unusually gullible?" Penny asked.

"I don't assume that people are lying to me," I replied.

"Lori's gullible," said Bree.

"That would explain it," said Penny, her frown vanishing. "She must have been teasing you." She stretched a placating hand across the table. "Try not to be cross with her. We old ladies must be allowed to behave like naughty schoolgirls from time to time. If nothing else, your wild goose chase has given us the pleasure of your company."

"The pleasure was ours," I said, fighting off an urge to hide my face. To be treated like a simpleton by a woman I respected was bad enough, but to be humiliated in front of strangers was beyond the limit. I felt like a complete idiot for believing Mrs. Craven and for dragging Bess and Bree to Old Cowerton to investigate her patently ridiculous confession.

"I believe we've said all we wished to say to you about Annabelle," said Penny. "Does anyone have anything else to add?"

When the other women shook their heads, Penny thanked them for coming and the party broke up. Susan, Gladys, Debbie, Alice, and Lorna gave me sympathetic nods or patted my arm consolingly before they left the conservatory. Their charitable gestures made me feel even more idiotic than I felt already.

Penny accompanied Bree and me to the front hall, where Nanny Sutton awaited us with Bess, who was sound asleep in the pram.

"She dropped off five minutes ago," Nanny Sutton informed me. "I tried to keep her awake, but . . ." She shrugged helplessly.

"It's okay," I said. "When my daughter needs a nap, she takes one, and there's nothing anyone can do about it. Thank you for looking after her."

"She's wonderful," said Nanny Sutton. "If

you need me again, please don't hesitate to call. Francesco has my number."

She hung back while Penny walked us to the door.

"Thank you for setting us straight about Annabelle," I told her.

"That's what friends are for," she said. "I can tell that you're Annabelle's friends. You wouldn't have come to Old Cowerton if you weren't."

I couldn't trust myself to speak, but Bree assured her that we thought the world of Annabelle.

"I hold private showings here five or six times a year," Penny went on. "If you leave your addresses, I'll see to it that you receive invitations. No purchase required," she emphasized. "Just come along for a spot of bubbly and some jollier conversations than the one we had today."

"It was the conversation we needed to hear," I said.

"Evidently," she said, smiling. "Please give Annabelle my best love. Tell her that I may own Craven Manor, but it will always be her home."

"I'll tell her," I promised, and as I wheeled my sleeping daughter down the retrofitted ramp, I promised myself that I'd tell Annabelle Craven a few other things as well. None of them complimentary.

Twenty-One

Bree and I made it all the way to Craven Manor's wrought-iron gates without exchanging a word. From the corner of my eye I could see her glance cautiously at me once or twice, but I was too mortified to look at her. I was also afraid of what I'd do if she so much as whispered "I told you so."

The gates swung open and we turned back toward the White Hart. Five more minutes passed before she worked up the courage to speak.

"I can feel you seething," she said.

"I can't imagine why," I said through gritted teeth.

She clamped her mouth shut and turned her head to survey the scenery on her side of the Rover before turning to me again and saying with unaccustomed humility, "I'm sorry I said you were gullible."

"Why should you be sorry?" I snapped. "It's obviously true."

"No, it's not," she said. "You trust people, that's all. It's one of the things I admire most about you."

"Have you ever seen me kick down a door?" I asked tersely. "Now, there's something to admire."

Bree wisely turned a chuckle into a cough.

"I wouldn't kick down Mrs. Craven's door," she advised. "She'll come back at you with a fistful of sewing needles."

"She's already punctured my pride." I gripped the steering wheel to keep myself from pounding it. "It'll be all over Finch by the time we get back, if it isn't already. 'I told Lori Shepherd I killed a man and she *believed* me!' What a jokester. Do you know how long it'll take me to live this down? Dick Peacock will leave a wild goose on my doorstep, I just know it."

"I'm sure he won't," Bree said soothingly. "We've all been the butt of jokes in Finch. You'll just have to laugh it off, pretend you don't mind."

"But I *do* mind," I said. "I wish I didn't, but I do. I've never been anything but kind to Mrs. Craven. Why would she pull such a mean prank on me?"

"I don't suppose the old-ladies-behaving-like-naughty-schoolgirls excuse will fly," said Bree.

"No, it won't," I said flatly. "She was bullied by schoolgirls when she was young and she didn't like it one bit." I released a furious breath and shook my head. "It'll be a long time before I forgive her."

"She may not have a long time," Bree pointed out.

"Then I may *never* forgive her," I barked. Bess shifted restlessly in her sleep and I lowered my voice to a determined murmur. "I think we should go back to Finch this afternoon."

"It's an option," Bree allowed, as though she were humoring a knife-wielding maniac. "But we've already paid for the suite and it would be a shame to waste our investment. Why don't we pack up tonight and head out in the morning?" She nudged me very gingerly with her elbow. "I could book a massage for you."

"I don't want a massage," I said sulkily.

"How about one last White Hart dinner?" she coaxed. "Crème brûlée is on the menu tonight. I checked."

"Crème brûlée?" I said, thawing slightly.

"Made with real vanilla beans, full-fat cream, and turbinado sugar," she crooned. "We still have some of Minnie's Melting Moments, too. You could have them later on, in front of the fire."

"Well," I said, my resistance dwindling, "I did tell Amelia that we might not be back until Friday."

"That's right," Bree said encouragingly. "It wouldn't be fair to descend on her without warning. She'll need time to say good-bye to Stanley. It won't be an easy parting for either of them. They're very close."

Entirely against my will, I began to laugh.

"First food, then emotional blackmail," I said. "I'd better give in before you turn on the tears." I wagged a reproving finger at Bree. "Don't think I don't know why you want us to spend another night in Old Cowerton. You think I need to chill out before I confront Annabelle."

"A cooling-off period wouldn't hurt," Bree said reasonably.

"I have a right to be miffed with her, don't I?" I demanded.

"Yes," said Bree, "but you'll set a bad example for your children if you kick her door down."

"Will and Rob would love it," I grumbled, but before she could remind me that ten-year-old boys weren't always the best judges of acceptable behavior, I surrendered. "Okay, you win. I'll make an effort to regain my composure tonight and we'll go home tomorrow."

"Yay!" Bree cheered. "Crème brûlée! Melting Moments!"

"And another Mariana massage?" I inquired with a grudging smile.

"No," she said happily. "A facial!"

I called Amelia as soon as we got back to the suite. She took the news of our imminent return in stride, as I'd known she would. While she and Stanley got along famously, she was well aware that his heart belonged to Bill.

I had no luck at all when I tried to call Bill. I could only assume that he and the boys were on a thrilling expedition to the farthest reaches of the Lake District, or that he'd forgotten to recharge his cell phone battery. I wasn't even moderately disappointed by my failure to speak with him. I was too hot under the collar to maintain the girls' getaway fiction, and I didn't think I could endure the gales of merry laughter that would greet a strictly factual account of my adventure.

When Bess woke from her nap, Bree and I took her and Moo for a last walk around Old Cowerton. We were accosted several times by friendly residents who beamed beatifically at my baby girl, but we eventually made it to St. Leonard's churchyard, where we searched for and found the four headstones that marked the final resting places of the men who'd loved Annabelle.

We paid our respects to Ted Fletcher, Jim Salford, William Walker May, and Edwin Craven, stopped in the church to say a prayer for their departed souls, and took a roundabout route back to the White Hart. We agreed that the town was quite beautiful and well worth a second visit, though I was honest enough to admit that a decent amount of time would have to pass before I set foot in it again.

After Bree left the suite for her facial, I settled Bess in the playpen and steeled myself to reveal the full extent of my ignominy to Aunt Dimity. I told myself that it would be therapeutic to express my feelings aloud to someone who had only my best interests at heart, but I still sat with the blue journal closed on my lap for several minutes before I mustered the moral fortitude to open it.

"Aunt Dimity?" I said. "It's been an utterly humiliating day."

I was too downcast to smile as the graceful lines of royal-blue ink appeared on the blank page.

It makes for a change from another strange

day, my dear. Were you stymied in your attempt to carry out the research I suggested?

"I didn't even try to carry out the research you suggested," I replied. "I didn't have to. Edwin Craven did it for me."

The late Edwin Craven?

"The deceased and dearly missed Edwin Craven," I confirmed. "His sister, Penelope Moorecroft, bought Craven Manor from Annabelle after Edwin's death. Penny invited Bree and me to join her and a few of Annabelle's old friends for brunch at Craven Manor this morning. While we feasted on caviar and Bess played in the knot garden, they systematically debunked each of the allegations we heard at Minnie's tea party. I guess you could call it the Craven Manor Crew versus the Sunnyside Gang."

Who won?

"The Craven Manor Crew, by a knockout," I said. "Penny has files Edwin compiled to refute every charge leveled against Annabelle. They prove her innocence way beyond a reasonable doubt. Edwin's files include eyewitness accounts given to the authorities by the women we met this morning."

Eyewitness accounts are preferable to rumors and innuendo, especially when accusations of murder are being bandied about.

"We heard them straight from the horses' mouths," I said. "Gladys Miller was picnicking with Annabelle when they and four other stunned bystanders saw Ted Fletcher trip and fall into the slurry pit. Debbie Lacey was hunting for mushrooms when she saw the riverbank collapse beneath Jim Salford's feet and send him tumbling into the rushing stream to drown. No one saw William Walker May's tragic accident, but Debbie argued persuasively that Annabelle couldn't have been responsible for it. Apart from that, the company that manufactured the heater in William Walker's greenhouse admitted liability."

Would I be correct in assuming that one of the women attending the brunch witnessed Edwin Craven's accident?

"You would," I said. "Penny Moorecroft was having a late-night chat with Annabelle, in Annabelle's bedroom, when Edwin rose from his sickbed. Penny was leaving Annabelle's room when she saw Edwin heading for the grand staircase. There was nothing she could do to prevent his fatal fall."

What happened to the vanishing sleeping tablets?

"They were filched by the nurse hired to look after Edwin," I said. "An investigation proved that she had a habit of stealing drugs from her patients and selling them online."

Despicable.

"Punishable by law as well," I said. "The nurse went to prison."

I should think so! Poor Annabelle. It seems that every time a good man came into her life, he died. I can understand why Minnie and her friends latched on to the idea of a widow's curse. In their view, she was being punished for the murder of her first husband.

"Except that she didn't murder her first husband, either," I said. "We come now to the grand finale." I felt an angry flush creep up my neck as I continued doggedly, "Alice Johnson and Lorna Small saw Zach Trotter walk away from Dovecote, unscathed, on the night of his alleged murder. After a lengthy search, Edwin Craven found Zach alive and as well as could be expected, drinking himself to death in an Australian bar. Annabelle didn't even have to have Zach declared dead. A long-distance divorce freed her to marry Edwin."

My goodness. It seems that Mrs. Craven lied to you.

"She lied through her *teeth* to me," I said heatedly. "She picked the easiest target in Finch and scored a bull's-eye. I'll bet she couldn't wait to tell everyone in the village about the hilarious trick she played on me at the quilting bee." I brought a fist down on the arm of the chair. "I believed her, Dimity! I actually struggled with the idea of turning her in to the police. I was so worried about Bill doing his duty as an officer of the court that I made up a cockamamie cover story to keep from telling him the truth, the whole truth, and nothing but the truth about our trip to Old Cowerton!"

I'm partly to blame, Lori. I'm afraid I encouraged you to go to Old Cowerton.

"I didn't need much encouragement," I reminded her. "I was ready and willing to pursue a perfectly pointless investigation. The Daft and Clueless Detective Agency, indeed. Bree may not be clueless, but I'm definitely daft. I'd have to be, to let myself believe, even for a minute, that Mrs. Craven could be a *serial killer*!" I clucked my tongue in disgust at my own idiocy. "I've never understood practical jokes, Dimity, and I've certainly never laughed at one, but to find myself the victim of a practical joke *Will* and *Rob* could have seen through is beyond demoralizing. I won't be able to show my face in the village for the next six months." I slumped disconsolately in my chair. "I must be the most naive nincompoop ever born."

Forgive me, Lori, but it doesn't seem like

the sort of thing Mrs. Craven would find amus-
ing. She's never played a practical joke on
you before, has she?

"Of course not," I said bitterly. "She
needed to gauge my level of gullibility
before she could spring one on me."

Ten years is an awfully long time to plan a
practical joke. In all the time you've known
her, has she ever teased you or taunted you
or made fun of you?

"No," I admitted gruffly. "Not to my face,
anyway."

Have you ever heard her make fun of any-
one else in Finch?

I paused for a moment to search my
memory, then said, "Now that you mention
it, I've never heard her make fun of anyone,
no matter where they live. It's not as if she's
prim or prudish. She smiles when people
crack jokes about Peggy Taxman, but she
doesn't toss off any zingers of her own." I
frowned down at the journal. "What are you
getting at, Dimity?"

A person's fundamental character doesn't
usually change overnight. In my experience, it
rarely changes at all. A querulous child will, in
most cases, grow up to be a querulous adult.

"The jealous girls in Annabelle's school
yard grew up to be jealous women," I said
reflectively.

Precisely. It would be as extraordinary for them to form an Annabelle Craven fan club as it would be for her to turn you into an object of derision.

I roused myself to sit upright as a gleam of hope shone through the stygian darkness of my despair. "Come to think of it, Dimity, she doesn't gossip, either. I bring her all sorts of juicy tidbits, but she never passes them on. The village grapevine withers and dies when it reaches Bluebell Cottage." I felt weak with relief as a new and glorious future began to glimmer on the horizon. "If Annabelle kept her little joke to herself, and if Bree doesn't give me away, I may be able to attend church without a bag over my head." I peered worriedly at the journal. "I don't think Bree will give me away. Do you, Dimity?"

While I appreciate your desire to avoid embarrassment, Lori, shouldn't you be asking yourself another question?

"I am," I said. "I'm asking myself if Mariana would accept a lucrative offer to move to Finch."

You needn't buy Bree's silence, Lori. She's your friend. What's more, she's a true-blue Kiwi. I can promise you that her sense of honor will prevail over her sense of humor.

"I'll have to tell Bill, though," I said, my

spirits plummeting. "He'll make jokes about cereal killers every time he empties a box of cornflakes."

You're forgetting that Bill loves you, Lori. He may allow himself a private chuckle at your expense every now and again, but he won't expose you to public ridicule.

"He is a pretty great guy," I agreed, bolstered by Aunt Dimity's comforting words. "I guess I can put up with a bit of razzing at home. Heaven knows I deserve it. I'd laugh at myself if I didn't feel like banging my stupid head against a wall."

Before you concuss yourself, my dear, I would urge you to answer one simple question.

"What question is that, Dimity?" I asked.

Why did Annabelle Craven lie to you?

I stared blankly at the simple question for so long that Aunt Dimity felt the need to rephrase it.

If Mrs. Craven didn't intend to play a mean-spirited trick on you, and if she isn't delusional, why would she go out of her way to convince you that she committed such a heinous crime?

"I have no idea," I said wonderingly. "And I still don't know what she buried beneath the rosebushes. I know it wasn't Zach, but what was it and why did she feel the need to bury it in the middle of the night?"

Your investigation is far from over, Lori. I suspect that the most intriguing chapter lies ahead of you.

"We're going home tomorrow," I said. "Bess and I will pay a call on Mrs. Craven as soon as we unpack." An image of the Rover's overloaded cargo compartment rose before my mind's eye, and I groaned softly as I added, "Which may take some time."

I shall be extremely interested to hear about your visit to Bluebell Cottage. You may come away from it feeling less foolish than you do now.

"I couldn't possibly feel *more* foolish," I pointed out.

One can always feel more foolish, my dear. But I don't think you will. In the meanwhile, try not to let your humiliating day spoil your final evening at the White Hart.

"I won't have to try too hard," I said, smiling a real smile for the first time since I'd opened the blue journal. "Crème brûlée is on the menu!"

Twenty-Two

As it turned out, crème brûlée wasn't on the menu. The head chef made it especially for me after Bree had a private word with him on her way to the hotel spa. Her clandestine scheme might have succeeded if she'd remembered to tell Erik and Lazlo that it was clandestine.

The truth was revealed when I thanked the two men for delivering yet another splendid dinner to the suite, whereupon Lazlo assured me that the chef was always ready to accommodate special requests. Bree's guilty face told me who'd made the special request and why, but she relaxed when she saw my grateful grin. I couldn't fault her for using whatever means she had at her disposal to chivy me into a less prickly mood. After we loaded the Rover, we spent the evening in perfect harmony, sharing Minnie's Melting Moments before the fire.

Bess saw to it that we got off to an early

start on Wednesday morning. Since I valued my wing mirrors, I let Erik drive the Rover through the narrow alleyway to a parking space in front of the hotel.

Francesco turned up after breakfast to escort us from the suite to our vehicle.

"Ciao, Francesco," Bree said as she climbed into the passenger seat. "*Mille grazie di tutto.* I've just used my entire Italian vocabulary, so please don't ask me to say anything else."

"*Prego,* madam," he said with a delighted smile. "Your accent is *molto buono.*" He waited for me to finish strapping Bess in her car seat, then opened the driver's door. When I was seated behind the wheel, he closed the door and said through the open window, "I think you came to Old Cowerton with many questions, madam. Please forgive me for asking, but . . . did you find the answers you were seeking?"

"I'm not sure yet," I said. "I'll let you know the next time I stay at the White Hart."

"I hope it will be very soon," he said. "You and *la piccola principessa* will always be welcome."

"What about me?" called Bree.

"But naturally, madam." Francesco spread his arms wide, as if to indicate that the

278

answer was self-evident. "Your fluency in my native tongue guarantees you a warm reception at the White Hart."

"You're a charmer, Francesco," said Bree, laughing. "Until next time!"

"Until then, madam." Francesco stood back and raised a hand in a farewell salute as we drove away.

"I'll miss him," Bree said with a wistful sigh.

"Not as much as you'll miss Mariana," I said.

"I'll miss them both equally," she said. "It's fun to be pampered."

"I could start calling you madam," I offered.

"I'd prefer *principessa*," she said.

"Sorry," I said. "I lack your grasp of Italian."

Bree whacked me on the arm, smiled sheepishly, and fell silent until we cruised past the entrance to the terraces.

"So," she said, "when do you plan to visit Mrs. Craven?"

"As soon as possible," I replied.

"Don't you dare go there without me," she warned.

"Wouldn't dream of it," I said. "I'll give you a ring as soon as Bess and I finish unloading the Rover."

Bree twisted around in her seat to peer at the cargo compartment, then faced forward again.

"I'll expect to hear from you sometime next week, then," she said.

"Sooner," I said, ignoring her unsubtle jibe. "We have to be done before Bill and the boys get home. Unloading two cars at once is a recipe for disaster."

We arrived in Finch an hour later and found it as splendidly somnolent as ever. James Hobson was scanning the village green with his metal detector, Mr. Barlow was repairing a downspout on the old schoolhouse, Sally Cook was watering the tulips in her window box, and Charles Bellingham was chatting with Christine Peacock on the doorstep of the Emporium. They each waved to us as we drove past, except for James Hobson, who was wearing headphones and gazing fixedly at the ground.

I glanced at the upstairs front window in Bluebell Cottage, but I didn't see Mrs. Craven in her workroom. I wondered if she was in the attic, selecting the fabrics she would use in her next baby quilt. I hoped she wasn't burying anything in her back garden.

I dropped Bree off at her mellow redbrick

house and continued up the lane, trying to remember what was in the refrigerator at home and debating whether or not I should have picked up a gallon of milk at the Emporium. I'd just decided that we hadn't been away long enough for the milk in the fridge to spoil when I saw a sight that drove all other thoughts from my mind.

Bill's car was parked in our gravel driveway. The trunk was open, but it hadn't been emptied, and the cargo carrier was still attached to the roof rack. I couldn't imagine why the intrepid outdoorsmen had cut their trip short, but I knew for a fact that my recipe for disaster was about to be tested.

I squeezed the Rover in beside Bill's Mercedes, released Bess from her car seat, and carried her into the cottage. A hubbub of familiar voices drew me to the kitchen, where I discovered my menfolk seated at the scrubbed pine table and chowing down on gargantuan sandwiches they'd apparently cobbled together from every leftover they could get their hands on.

"Mum!" Will and Rob chorused through bulging mouths.

I couldn't make out the rest of their greeting, but the hugs they gave me after they jumped to their feet rendered speech superfluous. Bess all but dove from my arms into

Bill's, and Stanley's powerful purr left me in no doubt that he was the happiest cat alive.

Chaos ensued.

The boys forgot their sandwiches in their eagerness to show me the collections of rocks, shells, sticks, feathers, bones, and interesting pieces of trash they'd amassed, all of which had to be unearthed from the jumble of dirty clothes festering in the overflowing car trunk. Each object prompted a story, and I had to listen to all of them while Bill changed Bess's diaper, fed her lunch, and rocked her to sleep in the relative serenity of the nursery.

When the boys ran out of stories to tell, I put them to work transferring the trunk's fetid contents to the laundry room. Bill eventually descended from the nursery to take charge of emptying the roof-mounted cargo carrier, but as soon as Will and Rob cleared the clothes from the trunk, I commandeered them to help me to unload the Rover.

We dropped things, tripped over things, and caromed off of one another like billiard balls. The sound of feet thundering up and down the stairs brought to mind cattle stampedes, but it didn't disturb my sleeping beauty. When Bess finished her nap, I put her in her playpen for her own safety.

I didn't aim for unpacking perfection, and I certainly didn't achieve it. By the time everything was in the general vicinity of where it belonged — including the tent, which Bill spread in the back meadow to dry — I was ready to wind down for the evening. Dinner was an informal affair, composed as it was of the leftover leftover sandwiches, reheated beef stew, and a batch of oatmeal cookies I dug out of the freezer and thawed in the microwave. The milk, thank heavens, was still drinkable.

It was close to midnight before Bill and I had a quiet moment to ourselves. With the children asleep upstairs and the last load of rancid laundry sloshing gently in the washing machine, we retreated to the living room with much-needed cups of tea. Bill collapsed into his favorite armchair and I lowered my weary body onto the sofa. Stanley's purr revved to new heights of contentment as he leapt onto Bill's knee and curled into a gleaming black ball on his lap.

"Welcome home," I said with a tired laugh.

"There's no place like it," he said, stroking Stanley's rumbling back. "Did you enjoy your getaway?"

"Did I enjoy having someone else prepare my meals, make my bed, and pick up after me in a lavish suite overlooking a walled garden? Hmm . . ." I peered at the fire in mock concentration, then shrugged nonchalantly. "Yeah, it was okay."

"Sounds like it," said Bill, smiling.

"Why did you come back early?" I asked. "I didn't expect to see you until Sunday."

"To be honest," he said, "the camping trip wasn't an unqualified success." He grimaced ruefully. "To be perfectly honest, it was a complete catastrophe. When the tent dries, I may set fire to it."

"I thought you were having a great time," I said, puzzled. "What went wrong?"

"What *didn't* go wrong?" he retorted. "Our campsite was in the middle of nowhere, it had no facilities of any kind, and it was as wet as a bog. We couldn't find a stick of dry firewood, so we couldn't make a fire. It rained so hard the second night that the tent collapsed on us and we had to sleep in the car. When the rain let up, the midges moved in. Then came the slugs."

"Ugh," I said, trying hard not to laugh.

"When we set the tent up again, it was covered with slugs," said Bill. "But we were so hungry by then that they almost looked appetizing."

"Lake District *l'escargot?*" I suggested.

"They were slugs, not snails," he said glumly. "And I didn't bring garlic or butter. I also forgot to pack the can opener, so we couldn't get at the baked beans or the soup, not that it mattered, because we couldn't build a fire to heat them."

"What did you eat?" I asked, fascinated.

"Energy bars and peanut butter sandwiches," he replied dully. "By day two, we were wet through and chilled to the bone, and we could hardly stand up straight because of the mud. When the tent collapsed a second time — possibly due to the weight of the slugs — I called it quits. We spent the next few days at a luxury hotel in Ullswater."

"Oh," I said as the penny dropped. "I wondered why the boys were raving about an indoor swimming pool."

"They spent most of their time in the pool," said Bill. "I spent most of mine in the hot tub, thawing out."

"Did you do *any* of the things you told me about on the phone?" I asked.

"Oh, yes," he said. "We hiked with a park ranger and we went fishing. We spotted a pair of ospreys, skipped stones on the lake, and rode the steam train in Ravenglass. The one thing we didn't do was go pony trek-

285

king. None of the local stables would allow it because half of the trails were flooded and the rest were hock-deep in mud. Which is why we came home early. The boys missed Thunder and Storm." He sighed. "And I missed my chair."

"Poor baby." I crossed to kiss him, then perched on the arm of his chair. "I'll help you with the tent bonfire. We can roast marshmallows."

"I'm afraid we'll end up roasting slugs," he said.

"At least you'll be rid of them," I said philosophically.

"Lori," he said, looking up at me, "the reason I didn't tell you the truth about —"

I interrupted him with another kiss. "You don't have to explain, Bill. In fact, I'm glad you were less than honest with me. You've paved the way for me to come clean about my girls' getaway."

"What happened?" he asked as I returned to the sofa. "Did you send a steak back to the kitchen because it was too rare?"

"We didn't send *anything* back to the kitchen," I said with a contented sigh. "The White Hart's chef is a genius."

"The meals at our hotel were superb, too," said Bill, "but Old Cowerton is a lot closer to Finch than Ullswater. Does the White

Hart accept reservations?"

"Bill," I said patiently, "I realize that you're preoccupied with food at the moment because you were forced to live on energy bars and peanut butter sandwiches for two whole days, but I'd be grateful if we could return to the subject at hand."

"Right," he said. "The truth about your girls' getaway. I'm all ears."

"Before I begin," I said, "I'd like to point out that I didn't laugh at your camping debacle."

"You wanted to," said Bill.

"I held it in," I said firmly. "I hope you'll afford me the same courtesy."

"What have you done, Lori?" he asked, the corners of his mouth twitching ominously.

"It's not so much what I've done," I temporized. "It's what I was led to believe." I took a deep breath and launched into a detailed and truthful account of everything that had happened since I'd taken a seat across from Annabelle Craven at the quilting bee.

I told him about her shocking confession, my uncertainty, and Aunt Dimity's suggestion that I look for answers in Old Cowerton. I told him about Bree's generous offer to accompany Bess and me. I recounted our initial conversation with Francesco, our alarming encounter with Bob Nash at the Willows Café, and my informative tête-à-tête with Hayley Calthorp at Nash's News.

After a short pause for a fortifying sip of tea, I went on to tell him about our visit to the terraces. I described the rosebushes in Dovecote's back garden, Susan Jessop's unexpected invitation, and Sunnyside's disturbingly suggestive floor plan. Finally, I summarized the startling accusations we heard at Minnie Jessop's tea party and the comprehensive refutations presented to us at Penny Moorecroft's brunch.

When I finished my long and tangled tale, Bill stared at me as if I'd sprouted antlers.

"Old Mrs. Craven?" he said incredulously. "A *serial killer?*"

"She wasn't always old," I protested. "And you have to admit that she left a trail of dead bodies in her wake."

"Yes, but —" He caught himself. "Sorry, Lori. I'm sure your suspicions made sense at the time."

"But that's the thing, Bill," I said earnestly. "My suspicions *didn't* make sense. None of it made sense. It still doesn't. Which is why I intend to visit Mrs. Craven tomorrow. I have to find out why she lied to me."

"I'd expect nothing less of you," he said.

"Take all the time you need. I'll look after the children. The boys will spend the day at the stables, naturally, but Bess and I have some catching up to do." He ducked his head, then gazed at me apologetically. "Sorry I wasn't entirely honest about my trip."

"I forgive you," I said. "Sorry I wasn't entirely honest about mine."

"I forgive you." Bill eased Stanley out of his lap, stood, and pulled me to my feet. "Now that we've proved what fine people we are, let's go to bed."

"I'll be up in a minute," I said. "I have to toss the clothes into the dryer."

"Don't be too long," he said, enfolding me in his arms. "Bess and I aren't the only ones who have some catching up to do."

TWENTY-THREE

After Bill, Bess, and the boys left for the stables the following morning, I telephoned Bree to let her know that I was ready to pay a call on Mrs. Craven. She feigned astonishment but agreed to be at her gate when I came by to pick her up at a quarter to ten.

In Finch, it was considered impolite to turn up on a neighbor's doorstep uninvited before ten o'clock. While I was miffed with Mrs. Craven, I remained too fond of her to treat her with disrespect.

I continued the laborious task of restoring order to the cottage until it was time for me to leave. Bree was in full Bree regalia when she joined me. Her short hair was again spiky, her jeans were torn artistically at the knees, her nose ring gleamed in the morning sun, and the skimpy tank top she wore beneath her black leather jacket would, I knew, reveal her tattooed arms.

We said very little as we cruised past Willis, Sr.'s wrought-iron gates and bumped over the humpbacked bridge, but when I parked the Rover in front of Bluebell Cottage, Bree found her voice.

"What's the plan?" she asked. "I hope it's not good cop–bad cop because I doubt that either one of us would make a very convincing bad cop. I may look the part, but Mrs. Craven knows what I'm really like. She's seen me play with Bess."

"Did you have chocolate pancakes for breakfast?" I asked, watching her closely. "Because you sound a little loopy. The plan, such as it is, couldn't be less complicated. We simply go in there and —" I broke off as Bree's dark eyes widened and darted from my face to a point just beyond my right shoulder. I swung around and found myself almost nose to nose with Annabelle Craven. I recoiled involuntarily, then smiled mechanically. She tapped on the window and I lowered it.

"Good morning, Lori," she said, beaming at me. "I heard you were back. And you brought Bree with you. How delightful! I'll set another place at the table. It won't take me a second. Come in, come in!"

"*Another* place at the table?" Bree murmured as Mrs. Craven disappeared into Bluebell Cottage. "Why did she set the table to begin with? Did you let her know you were coming?"

"I haven't spoken with her since the quilting bee," I said.

"It must be another ambush tea party," said Bree. "Why are these old ladies always a step ahead of us?"

"They have spy networks," I said sagely, "and they know how to use them."

Mrs. Craven was waiting for us in her dining room. A tall stack of newly completed baby quilts occupied one end of the mahogany table — one of the "few sticks of furniture" Penny Moorecroft had mentioned — while the far end was draped with an aging but immaculate linen tablecloth.

As we entered the room, Mrs. Craven was adding a third place setting to the two she'd already arranged around her familiar bone china tea service and a serving dish piled high with Melting Moments. I wondered if Minnie Jessop had given her the recipe before Zach Trotter's departure had cast a shadow over their relationship.

"Please, have a seat," Mrs. Craven said cheerfully. "I filled the pot as soon as I saw you come over the bridge. The tea should be steeped to perfection by now."

She took her place at the head of the table and gestured for us to take the other two.

Bree sat on her left and I sat on her right, facing each other across the spotless expanse of linen. Mrs. Craven filled our cups and urged us to help ourselves to the treats she'd provided, then folded her hands and leaned toward me, her gray eyes twinkling.

"I've been expecting you," she said. "Are you going to have me arrested?"

"N-no," I stammered, caught off guard.

"Why not?" she inquired, sounding both curious and disappointed. "You went to Old Cowerton, didn't you?"

"Yes," I replied.

"And you spoke with Minnie Jessop," she continued.

"How do you know we spoke with Minnie Jessop?" Bree interjected.

"Hayley Calthorp rang me," said Mrs. Craven. "Hayley knows everything that goes on in Old Cowerton."

"Then she must know that we spoke with your sister-in-law as well," I said.

"Oh, dear," said Mrs. Craven, her face falling. "I might have known that Penny would put a spanner in my spokes. I suppose she told you that I didn't murder Zach."

"She and her friends made it clear that you didn't murder anyone," I said.

"I'm sure they meant well," Mrs. Craven

said, looking a bit cross, "but I do wish they hadn't interfered."

"Interfered with what?" I asked, bewildered. "You don't *want* to be arrested, do you?"

"But that's exactly what I *do* want," Mrs. Craven replied. "I don't suppose you could ignore what Penny told you, as a favor to me? Surely Minnie's story is more persuasive than the one Penny offered."

"It may have been persuasive," I said, "but it wasn't true, was it?"

"No," Mrs. Craven admitted reluctantly. "It wasn't."

"I think it's about time you told us the truth," said Bree. "You may not owe it to me, but you owe it to Lori. You have no idea how worried she was after you lied to her about Zach, or how stupid she felt for taking you seriously."

"I'm sorry, my dear," said Mrs. Craven, gazing contritely at me. "I'm afraid I chose you because I knew you'd take me seriously. It's one of the reasons, at any rate."

"Happy to oblige," I muttered, wondering if everyone in Finch had me pegged as a soft touch.

"Just tell us the truth, Mrs. Craven," Bree insisted. "Tell us what really happened on the night Zach Trotter left you."

"I've never told anyone before," she said, "except Edwin. He thought I was a fool to protect Zach, but I couldn't give him away. I was his wife."

"Zach's probably in a place where he doesn't need your protection anymore," Bree said gently. "He was well on his way there when Edwin found him in Australia."

"It wasn't his fault," Mrs. Craven said abruptly. "The drinking, the thieving — none of it was his fault. The war damaged him. He couldn't leave it behind. He couldn't stop dodging bullets. Taking risks made him feel alive, and drinking blurred the memories of the unspeakable sights he'd seen on the battlefield."

It was a view of Zach I hadn't considered, and I felt ashamed of myself for being so shortsighted.

"I was in bed when he came home that night," Mrs. Craven began. "I heard him come in. I heard him stagger upstairs. I heard him stumble at the top of the stairs and I heard the most awful noise. I sprang out of bed, terrified that I would find him injured or perhaps dead, but Zach hadn't fallen."

"What had fallen?" Bree asked.

"His ill-gotten gains," Mrs. Craven replied, looking down at her folded hands.

"On his way home from the pub, he robbed the church. He stole the processional candlesticks from St. Leonard's, the tall ones they use during the Easter Vigil. It's a miracle no one saw him with them. He intended to hide them under our bed, but he dropped them when he reached the landing. There were two of them, each of them four feet tall and gold plated. They made a dreadful racket tumbling down the stairs."

"Minnie described it as a sort of bump-thud-rumbling noise," I said.

"I'd say it was more of a clang than a rumble," Mrs. Craven said judiciously, "but it would have sounded different to Minnie, hearing it through the wall."

"What happened next?" Bree asked, riveted.

"I was a faithful churchgoer," said Mrs. Craven. "The vicar trusted me to repair his vestments. I couldn't allow my husband to desecrate St. Leonard's, but I couldn't turn him in to the police, either."

"Tough choice," Bree commented. "How did you get around it?"

"I told Zach to leave town and never to come back," Mrs. Craven answered, with a slight tremble in her voice. "I'd forgiven his trespasses time and time again, but there are some trespasses God alone can forgive.

After he left, I rolled the candlesticks in a rug to muffle the sound and hid them in the trench I'd dug for my rosebushes."

"Minnie saw you hide them," I told her.

"I know," said Mrs. Craven. "Her misinterpretation of events was an unexpected complication, but not an insuperable one. The constable who questioned me didn't care for Minnie. She'd spread a dreadful rumor about his auntie a few years earlier, so I had no trouble convincing him that I was a wronged woman — wronged by my nosy neighbor as well as by my runaway husband. He poked around the rosebushes for appearances' sake, but he didn't order me to dig them up."

"Are the candlesticks still there?" I asked.

"Certainly not," said Mrs. Craven, looking shocked. "They belonged to the church."

Bree eyed her with amused disbelief. "You didn't return them, did you?"

"Of course I did," Mrs. Craven replied. "A month or so later, after the to-do surrounding the theft had died down, I dug them up and smuggled them back into St. Leonard's, wrapped in a chasuble I'd hemmed for the vicar. I hung the chasuble in the vestry and hid the candlesticks in a dark corner near the entrance to the crypt.

When they were discovered a few days later, it was assumed they'd been mislaid. The investigation ceased and I breathed a sigh of relief. I also said many prayers of contrition for my dishonesty and for my failure as a wife."

"Your failure as a wife?" Bree exploded. "I would have given Zach the boot a lot sooner than you did."

"Edwin said much the same thing," said Mrs. Craven, smiling. "He would have liked you, Bree. He admired strong women."

"I wish I'd known him," said Bree.

My young friend shared a moment of quiet reflection with my elderly friend, but I was still miffed.

"Okay," I said a little too loudly. "You've told us the true story behind Zach's departure, and for that I thank you. But why in God's name did you try to con me into believing that you killed him?"

Mrs. Craven ran a finger around the rim of her teacup, then said, half to herself, "I never expected to live this long."

"Sorry?" I said uncomprehendingly.

"I've used up nearly all of the fabric I brought with me when I moved to Finch," she went on. "The bins in my attic are empty. But even if I had an endless supply of fabric, I would still have to face the fact that I will soon have no place to store it."

"What are you talking about?" Bree asked.

"I've run out of money, my dear," said Mrs. Craven. "When I visited my bank manager last week, he alerted me to the sorry state of my finances."

"How can your finances be in a sorry state?" Bree demanded. "Edwin was rich, wasn't he? And Penny must have paid you a packet for Craven Manor."

"He was and she did," Mrs. Craven acknowledged, "but I spent a great deal on the care Edwin received during his final illness. The experimental drugs and the various therapies drained our resources. I thought that, by selling the manor and living more simply in a much smaller house, I would have sufficient funds to see me through to the end of my days." She smiled ruefully. "Unfortunately, my days have gone on rather longer than I anticipated." She looked earnestly from me to Bree. "It can happen to anyone, my dears, so I urge you to plan ahead. It's a terrible mistake to outlive one's bank balance."

"How bad is it?" I asked.

"I'm afraid my financial motorcar is running on fumes," she replied. "I shall soon have to give up Bluebell Cottage and become a ward of the state. The best I can hope for is a bed in a state-run rest home for the elderly."

Bree and I began to protest, but she held up a hand to silence us.

"I contemplated a variety of alternatives," she said. "Living under a bridge in London, for example, or taking to the road with a small pack on my back. Both ideas seemed feasible until I remembered the vagaries of English weather. It would be one thing to sleep rough on a fine summer night. It would be something else entirely during a cold snap in late January."

Bree and I exchanged appalled glances, then looked at Mrs. Craven again.

"I turned my mind to alternatives that included room and board," she went on, "but it seemed unlikely that the army would allow me to enlist or that I could find work as a live-in servant. As you know, live-in servants are all but unheard of these days. Nothing practicable occurred to me until the day of the quilting bee." Her eyes began to dance. "The bee was to be my farewell gift to Finch. I couldn't have known that it would present me with an eminently sensible solution to my problem."

I gazed at her raptly as she paused to sip her tea.

"I don't know if you'll recollect it," she

said, "but at some point during the bee the conversation turned to the topics of prisons and prisoners. All at once, it struck me that I might use my dubious past to make my future more bearable. After that, it was a case of one thing leading to another. You and I were alone at the quilt frame, Lori. I was aware of your trusting nature, just as I was aware of your husband's profession."

"You knew I'd buy into your story," I guessed, "and you hoped I'd tell Bill."

"If all had gone according to plan," said Mrs. Craven, "Bill would have been obliged to notify the authorities, and I would have been placed under arrest for murder." She heaved a regretful sigh. "I grossly underestimated your thirst for the truth."

"Why would you want to be arrested for a crime you didn't commit?" I asked, mystified.

"Because I'd rather spend the rest of my life in prison than in a rest home for the elderly," Mrs. Craven replied.

"You've got to be joking," said Bree.

"I'm not," said Mrs. Craven. "State-run homes do their best, but the government is constantly cutting their funding." There wasn't the faintest hint of self-pity in her voice as she continued matter-of-factly, "Old people don't count for much in this country. We aren't productive citizens. To the contrary, we're a burden on society. It would be better for all concerned if we died quickly and quietly, but some of us are doomed to go on living well past our sell-by date."

"We wouldn't allow you to live in a place that didn't look after you properly," I said, recalling the minimal care Minnie's friends received at Newhaven.

"I wouldn't want to live in a well-run home, either," said Mrs. Craven. "Edwin's nursing home was positively luxurious but even if I could afford it, I wouldn't want to live there."

"Why not?" Bree asked.

"I spent my youth surrounded by death," said Mrs. Craven. "I lost Ted, Jim, and William Walker after the war, but I lost many more friends during it. I don't want to be surrounded by death in my old age as well — and nothing is more certain in a rest home than death. Apart from that, there's the tedium. It would be desperately dull to be confined to a place filled with people my own age, a place where every waking hour is regulated by a rigid schedule. I wouldn't be able to exchange everyday pleasantries with your lovely young man, Bree. I wouldn't see Will and Rob play cricket on the green, and I'd be deprived of the pleasure of watching them teach Bess how to bowl. I wouldn't hear Mr. Barlow argue with Mr. Peacock over fripperies, and I'd never again hear Mrs. Taxman lay down the law at a committee meeting. A woman as forthright as Mrs. Taxman would undoubtedly be sedated."

"Undoubtedly," Bree murmured.

"Finch may appear to be a quiet village," Mrs. Craven went on, "but it's bursting with life in all its wonderful variety. It's anything but tedious."

"I agree with you," I said, "and I understand why you'd hate to leave Finch. But I still don't understand why you'd prefer prison to a rest home."

"I think I do," said Bree. "Shall I have a go at explaining it, Mrs. Craven?"

"Give it your best shot, my dear," said Mrs. Craven.

Bree leaned back in her chair and favored Mrs. Craven with a speculative gaze before saying thoughtfully, "In prison, you'd be housed, fed, and clothed, but above all, you wouldn't be bored. You'd meet all sorts of people from all walks of life, and each one of them would have a different story to tell. The schedule would still be pretty rigid, but there'd be no lack of spontaneity. There'd

303

be fistfights and food fights and salty language and secret romances and tons of gossip. Life in prison might be dangerous, but it wouldn't be dull." She cocked her head toward our hostess. "How am I doing?"

"I couldn't have put it better myself," Mrs. Craven replied, "though I would reiterate that it would be a constant source of heartache to make new friends only to watch them pass away, an inevitable occurrence in a rest home for the elderly. In prison, I might lose friends to parole or to the odd stabbing in a shower stall, but I imagine most of them would be around for a good long while. They might even visit me after they were released!" She clasped her hands together, as if nothing could possibly please her more than prison visits from ex-cons. "I'd also add that my age would probably preclude my incarceration with violent offenders. Then, too, there's the prospect of occupational therapy. State-run homes rarely have the budget for it, but I'm told it's all the rage in prison. I doubt that I'd be allowed to carry on with my quilting — scissors and needles might be a cause for concern among the guards — but I could learn a new skill. Pottery, perhaps. Wet clay is harmless, isn't it? I could learn to make little pots."

I stared at her, torn between exasperation and a powerful desire to giggle.

"Annabelle," I said, "prison isn't like summer camp. If you were convicted of murder, you'd be treated very severely."

"At least I'd be treated with respect," she retorted. "I wouldn't be subjected to the baby talk reserved for the elderly." Her voice became cloyingly patronizing. " 'Have we taken our medication today?' 'Would we like a pat of butter on our toast?' 'Do we need to visit the loo?' " She snorted. "I'm old! I'm not addled!"

"You tell 'em, Mrs. Craven," Bree declared, slapping the table.

"No one who knows you thinks you're addled, Annabelle," I said. "And no one — absolutely no one — thinks of you as a burden. Penny would jump for joy if you moved in with her at Craven Manor."

"Oh, no," Mrs. Craven said, shaking her head. "I can't go back to Craven Manor. I wouldn't mind it so much if Edwin's ghost roamed the corridors. It's his absence I can't stand. Every time I passed the great staircase, I would see his broken body and remember the blood." She shuddered. "I'm sorry, Lori, but I couldn't possibly return to Craven Manor. I'd be going back to a time I can't bear to revisit."

"Good," said Bree. "I'd just as soon you stay in Bluebell Cottage."

"There's nothing I'd like more, Bree," said Mrs. Craven. "But I can't afford it, and I won't accept charity, regardless of —"

"Who said anything about charity?" Bree interrupted. "I'll see to it that you pay your own way."

"We both will," I said promptly, though I couldn't fathom what scheme Bree had up her sleeve.

"How?" asked Mrs. Craven.

"Leave it to us," said Bree. "We'll have you back on your feet again before you can say Pentonville."

"You're one of us, Annabelle," I said staunchly. "And in Finch, we look after our own."

"Well," said Mrs. Craven, looking dazed, doubtful, and hopeful all at once. "I suppose it would be self-serving of me to wish you luck, but . . ." A radiant smile highlighted every crease in her gloriously wrinkled face. "Good luck!"

Twenty-Four

The old schoolhouse was packed with people. The villagers were there, of course, as were our local farming families, but seven seats in the front row were occupied by first-time visitors to Finch. Penny Moorecroft, Susan Jessop, Gladys Miller, Debbie Lacey, Lorna Small, Alice Johnson, and Hayley Calthorp had no idea how utterly bizarre it was to see Bree Pym and Peggy Taxman sitting side by side behind the table on the dais.

The only villager absent from the proceedings was Annabelle Craven. Bill, Bess, and the boys had spirited her away to see the drifts of daffodils at Hidcote Manor. Bill was under strict orders to keep Mrs. Craven at a safe distance from Finch until I telephoned to let him know that the coast was clear.

Two days had passed since Mrs. Craven had revealed her dilemma to Bree and me.

I'd spoken with her landlord, who'd readily agreed to reduce her rent to a token sum, but Bree had devised a rescue plan of such scope and magnificence that it took my breath away. The next hour would determine its success or ensure its failure.

Grant Tavistock and Charles Bellingham, who were conversing animatedly with Penny Moorecroft, resumed their seats when Peggy Taxman banged the gavel. A hush fell over the room, but it was instantly shattered by Peggy's voice.

"I hereby call an extraordinary meeting of the village affairs committee to order," she boomed. "I gladly yield the floor to Bree Pym."

Since Peggy rarely yielded the floor to anyone, gladly or otherwise, the silence in the room deepened. The air seemed to vibrate with suspense as Bree rose to her feet and walked to the front of the dais to gaze wordlessly from one upturned face to the next. When every pair of eyes was focused on her, she spoke.

"Mrs. Craven's in trouble," she said. "She's in trouble because her husband got sick and she didn't. When her husband got sick, she spent a lot of money to make him better, but all the money in the world couldn't buy a cure for Alzheimer's."

The older villagers shifted uncomfortably in their seats, as if the mere mention of the disease filled them with dread.

"After her husband died," Bree continued, "Mrs. Craven went on living. She had to make a few changes because she couldn't afford to live the way she used to, but she didn't mind. Bluebell Cottage became her new home. You became her new family." Bree began to pace slowly back and forth across the dais, her gaze lingering first on one person, then on another. "She gave you cups of sugar when you needed them. She watered your plants and fed your pets when you were away. She listened to your stories and she laughed at your jokes. She always had a smile ready when she ran into you on the village green or in church or at the Emporium or during a deadly dull committee meeting."

Peggy's gimlet gaze fixed beadily on Bree, and some of the braver villagers chuckled, but the rest nodded affectionately as they recalled their everyday encounters with Mrs. Craven.

"As Mrs. Craven went on living, she made quilts," said Bree. "She sold them at the fete to raise money for St. George's. Mr. Barlow will tell you what a difference the new drainage system has made in the churchyard. The vicar will tell you how much more pleasant it is to greet us in the south porch, now that the roof doesn't leak. And I don't think any of us miss the lytch-gate's rusty old hinges."

"I don't," Sally Cook declared. "I could hardly open the gate before the new hinges were installed."

A round of vigorous nods supported her claim.

"We owe Mrs. Craven more debts of gratitude than I can count," said Bree. "But even if we didn't owe her a thing, we'd owe it to ourselves to help her out. As a wise friend of mine said just the other day: Mrs. Craven is one of us, and in Finch, we look after our own."

Having felt profoundly unwise for the past several days, I ducked my head, embarrassed by Bree's praise. Meanwhile, Peggy eyed the room belligerently, as if daring anyone to contradict her chosen speaker.

"What's the problem, Bree?" Mr. Barlow called.

"The problem," Bree replied, "is that Mrs. Craven isn't dead."

Her blunt description of Mrs. Craven's predicament provoked a confused murmur and in some cases dark looks of disapproval, but Bree merely waited for the clamor to die down before she went on.

"We all believe a long life is a good thing," she said. "We raise our glasses to it in the pub. We wish it for our children. We pray for it in church. Mrs. Craven's been blessed with the long life we all hope for. The problem is, she's outlived her savings. If we don't do something, and do it right away, she'll be carted off to live in the kind of place we don't even want to visit."

Several people began to speak at once, but Bree held up both her hands for silence.

"She's too proud to accept charity, so it's no good passing the hat," she said. "I have a plan that will enable Mrs. Craven to support herself, but it'll take all of us to make it work."

"Just tell us what to do," said Grant Tavistock.

"We sell her quilts," said Bree, "and I'm sorry, Mr. Bunting, but we don't donate the profits to St. George's."

"I wouldn't hear of it," the vicar said indignantly.

"I know you wouldn't, Mr. Bunting. We all do." Bree gave him a reassuring smile, then nodded at Emma Harris, who sat beside me. "I've already spoken with Emma. Before she started her riding school, Emma was a professional software designer. She's agreed to design and to implement an online campaign targeted at quilt collectors across the globe."

A rumble of approval rippled through the room, and Christine Peacock leaned forward to clap Emma on the shoulder.

"The market for handmade quilts is very healthy at the moment," Emma said to the room at large. "Collectors demand authenticity, and no one is more authentic than Mrs. Craven. The prices they're willing to pay will make your eyes pop."

"You've brought up a good point, Emma," said Bree. "Before we sell the quilts, we have to figure out a fair market price for them. That's where Grant and Charles come in. They make a living valuing art — and I think we can all agree that Mrs. Craven's quilts qualify as art."

"I framed mine," said Hayley Calthorp.

"So did I," I chimed in.

"They're art of the highest quality," Charles proclaimed. "Mrs. Craven sold them for a fraction of their worth. Grant and I will see to it that her works are priced fairly."

"You can also use your connections in London to get them into high-end shops," said Bree.

"Leave that part to me," said Penny. She

rose from her front-row seat and turned to address the assembly. "My name is Penelope Moorecroft. I'm Annabelle Craven's sister-in-law, and because I have lots of grandchildren and great-grandchildren, I'm known in every fashionable children's boutique in London. I'll have no trouble persuading the owners to sell Annabelle's quilts at boutique prices."

"We'll contact art museums," said Grant. "I wouldn't be at all surprised to see a bidding war break out over Mrs. Craven's masterpieces."

"I can help there as well," said Penny.

"Mrs. Moorecroft is a well-known sculptor," Bree put in, for the benefit of those who were unaware of Penny's profession.

"I'm personally acquainted with quite a few museum directors as well as a number of influential gallery owners," Penny said. "If they wish to display my work or to be invited to my open houses in future, they'll join the bidding war."

Charles and Grant saluted her amid general applause, and she resumed her seat. Looking a bit disgruntled, Sally Cook spoke up.

"I'm not a computer expert," she said, "and I don't shop in hoity-toity boutiques. I've never set foot in an art gallery, and I wouldn't recognize a museum curator unless he was wearing a name tag that said 'Hello, I'm a Museum Curator.' What can people like me do to help Mrs. Craven?"

"For a start, you can help her to refill her fabric bins," said Bree. "No tatty scraps, please. Don't bring her any cloth you wouldn't want to see in a quilt made for a child you love."

"Old cotton," said Mr. Barlow. "It's what she prefers."

"I'll turn out my cupboards," said Christine Peacock, "and have a good rummage in the charity shops."

"I'll look through the bins at the needlework store in Upper Deeping," said Emma, who was as proficient at knitting as she was at everything else. "They always have offcuts for sale."

"There's something else we can all do," said Bree. "I'm willing to bet that most of the people who bought Mrs. Craven's quilts at the fete were aware that she was selling them for a pittance."

"I bought my quilts from her when she lived in Old Cowerton," said Hayley Calthorp. "I wanted to pay her more, but she wouldn't accept it. Annabelle's always been too modest for her own good."

"You're right about that," said Bree, "but

we can be brazen on her behalf."

"How?" Sally asked.

"If you know people who bought Mrs. Craven's quilts in the past," said Bree, "you can try to persuade them to chip in a little extra, to bring the price closer to what it should have been in the first place. Some of them will look the other way, but others — the ones with a functioning conscience — may be open to the idea."

"It's worth a try," said Sally. "It might even be fun. I'm not afraid to play the guilt card in a good cause."

I could see Elspeth Binney, Opal Taylor, Millicent Scroggins, and Selena Buxton sit up and take notice when Sally mentioned the guilt card. The Handmaidens were singularly adept at haggling. They had no compunction about employing guilt as a means to achieve their ends. I almost pitied the quilt owners they would visit.

"We'll see what we can do in Old Cowerton," said Lorna Small, and the rest of the Craven Manor Crew nodded emphatically.

"You might even find people willing to sell the quilts back to us at their original prices," Bree added. "The more of those people you find, the better. If Mrs. Craven's quilts take off, she may not be able to keep up with the demand."

"She won't have to," Charles said confidently. "Rarity increases value. It's not always true, of course, but in this case, it is. I agree that it would be helpful to have a backlog of quilts, but with the proper positioning and promotion, Mrs. Craven should be able to live quite comfortably on no more than ten or twelve quilt sales a year."

"Five or six, if I have anything to do with it," Penny interjected.

"Lori and I saw a big stack of finished quilts on her dining room table when we were at her house on Thursday," said Bree. "She's getting them ready for the fete."

"It's time for us to get to work, then," said Grant.

"We'll have to take photographs of the quilts," said Emma, "and write up an appealing biography."

"I wonder if we could persuade her to name her quilts?" Elspeth Binney asked. "It would add a storybook touch."

"She'll think it's a very silly thing to do," said Bree, "but if we ask her nicely, she might do it."

"We'll take a portrait photograph of Mrs. Craven to go along with the biography," Charles said. "Her face guarantees her authenticity."

"I can set up the quilt frame again, and you can take snaps of her working at it," Mr. Barlow suggested.

"Why not film her working at the quilt frame?" said Henry Cook. "Emma will know how to post it online."

"Brilliant!" Elspeth exclaimed.

"I saw a basket filled with old cotton aprons at the charity shop last week," said Christine. "I'm sure Mrs. Craven will be able to do something with them." She stood and bellowed, "Who wants to come with me to Upper Deeping?"

From that point on, the meeting was up for grabs. Lilian Bunting, Sally Cook, and Felicity Hobson joined Christine Peacock's charity shop expedition. Charles Bellingham and Grant Tavistock swept Emma Harris off to meet Penny Moorecroft. The Handmaidens and the Craven Manor Crew came together to compare wheedling techniques. Everywhere I looked I saw knots of people discussing ways to build on Bree's ideas. I'd seldom been prouder of my village.

To my very great astonishment, Peggy Taxman allowed the creative free-for-all to continue without her guidance. She gave the gavel a feeble tap, then shook her head and joined her husband and the vicar to decide how best to replace Mrs. Craven's stall at the upcoming church fete.

Bree jumped down from the dais and stood beside me to survey her handiwork.

"How did you get Peggy to keep her mouth shut?" I asked quietly.

"I promised not to disrupt her meetings for the next six months," Bree replied. "I'm afraid Bess and I will have to take our games of Big Bad Bear outside for a while."

"The fresh air will do her good," I said. "You have to hand it to Peggy, though. She hit the nail on the head when she called today's meeting extraordinary. I've never seen anything like it. Your plan for saving Mrs. Craven is off and running."

"Do you think it'll work?" Bree asked.

"With a truly wise woman at the helm," I said, nudging her with my elbow, "how can it fail?"

EPILOGUE

In the end, Bill decided not to burn the tent. After some deliberation — and a good night's sleep — he realized that the tent's immolation would send the wrong message to the boys and quite possibly poison them as it released toxic fumes into the atmosphere.

Instead of roasting marshmallows over his bête noire, we cleaned it up and returned it to the attic with the rest of the camping gear. If more than an inch of dust accumulates on the gear, we've agreed to donate it to the charity shop in Upper Deeping. I'll be up there with a ruler next April.

Like me, Bill prefers to rough it at the White Hart. After leaving the children with Willis, Sr., and Amelia, he and I spent a long weekend there a few weeks after my first visit to Old Cowerton. Francesco greeted us like old friends and made sure that everything was arranged perfectly for us in the honeymoon suite.

We left a big tip for red-haired Megan after she served us omelets at the Willows Café. We stopped in Nash's News to hear the latest gossip from Hayley Calthorp. We had a cup of tea with Minnie and Susan Jessop at Sunnyside, and we spent several pleasant hours with Penny Moorecroft at Craven Manor.

Before we left Old Cowerton, we dropped by Newhaven to deliver a basket of baked goods to Mildred, Myrtle, and Mabel. I was unimpressed with the level of hygiene as well as the medical care I found there, but as I told Bill, if we visit the places we don't want to visit, we may force the people who run them to run them better.

When Bree's partner, Jack MacBride, returned from his lecture tour in Scandinavia, she roped him into helping her run the Saving Mrs. Craven Campaign, as it came to be called. Jack's main contribution was a pair of strong legs, which he put to good use hauling fabric bins up and down from Mrs. Craven's attic. The bins came down empty but went up full, thanks to the villagers' copious contributions of old cotton cloth.

No one who owned a precampaign baby

quilt was willing to sell it back to Mrs. Craven, but nearly everyone was willing to pay the difference between the pittance she'd charged and the fair market value. I was the first to pay my share. I would have paid twice as much to keep Sally Cook and the Handmaidens from descending on me, armed with the guilt card.

Though she thought it was very silly indeed, Mrs. Craven put up with the photo shoot in the old schoolhouse, and the charming video Henry Cook made of her using the quilt frame quickly went viral. No matter how nicely we asked her, however, she refused to name her quilts, nor would she allow anyone else to name them.

"They already have names," she insisted. "Old Maid's Ramble, Johnny 'Round the Corner, Tumbling Blocks, Broken Dishes . . . If those names were good enough for the generations of quilters who came before me, they're good enough for me."

Thanks to the efforts of Bree, Emma, Penny, Charles, Grant, and many others, Mrs. Craven has become a star in the quilting firmament. The bidding wars Grant predicted continue to take place, mainly online. When Emma told me how much money the first online auction brought in, I was compelled to admit that computers had their uses.

Even after Grant and Charles brought Mrs. Craven to see one of her quilts displayed in a museum, she couldn't take her newfound status as an artist seriously.

"I think she'd still rather see her quilts stained, torn, and dragged through the mud by a toddler," I said, looking down at the blue journal.

The study was still and silent. Bill was at his office in Finch, Will and Rob were in school, Stanley was asleep in Bill's armchair, and Bess was enjoying a siesta in the nursery. Autumn sunlight fell softly through the strands of ivy crisscrossing the diamond-paned windows above the old oak desk, casting tangled shadows on the tall bookshelves. I smiled as the graceful lines of royal-blue ink unfurled across the blank page in a response Mrs. Craven would have appreciated.

Of course she would, Lori. The best-loved quilts tend to be used until they fall apart. What greater compliment could Mrs. Craven receive than to see her quilts loved to pieces?

"She certainly seems impervious to other kinds of compliments," I commented. "She can't understand why so many of us pitched in to help her. She puts it down to our goodness rather than hers."

I was privileged to meet quite a few good people in my lifetime, Lori, and none of them thought of themselves as good. They didn't consider themselves bad people, but they were aware of their flaws and they strove constantly to overcome them. Mrs. Craven might regard her reluctance to revisit her friends in Old Cowerton as a flaw.

"If she does, she's striving to overcome it," I said. "She hasn't yet returned to Old Cowerton, and she may never return to Craven Manor, but she's welcomed Penny, Susan, Gladys, and the rest of her old friends to Bluebell Cottage. She even invited Minnie to visit her!"

Has Minnie accepted the invitation?

"No," I said, "but after Bill and I told her about the theft that prompted Zach's disappearance, she said she might rethink her opinion of Annabelle."

Good for Minnie! It's not easy to reject a story one has believed for decades, especially when that story has been one's claim to fame.

"Minnie's Melting Moments are a much better claim to fame," I said. "Annabelle served them at the unveiling of the Star of Bethlehem quilt in St. George's on Sunday."

Ah, yes, the quilt everyone helped to quilt at the quilting bee. I presume Mrs. Craven turned down the vicar's offer to purchase it.

"She insisted on donating it to the church," I said. "She says the quilting bee quilt belongs in St. George's because it reflects the spirit of the community. All I can say is, if our wonky stitches reflect our community, then Finch is in deep trouble."

I don't think Mrs. Craven would agree with you, Lori. I think she would say that Finch got her out of trouble.

"We freed her from the widow's curse of an impoverished old age," I said. "What kind of a world drives a woman like Mrs. Craven to think that she would be better off as a prisoner than as a pensioner?"

You'll go mad if you worry about the whole world, my dear. If you must think in global terms, think of kindness as a ripple that spreads outward. If you wish to make the world a better place, send out as many ripples as you can.

"Bree made a great big splash of kindness," I said.

She'd be the first to tell you that she didn't do it alone. Finch came together to help Mrs. Craven. When she looks at the quilt's wonky stitches, I suspect she sees nothing but love.

"I hope so," I said, but as I thought of my neighbors and their selfless efforts to save Mrs. Craven, I knew in my heart that Aunt

Dimity was right. Friendships, like quilts, brought warmth and comfort to our lives. Our stitches might not be perfect, but they were as strong as the love that united us in the crazy quilt we called home.

MINNIE'S MELTING MOMENTS

Ingredients

1 cup all-purpose flour
1/2 cup cornstarch
1/2 cup confectioners' sugar
3/4 cup butter

Directions

1. Combine dry ingredients.
2. Cream butter until fluffy.
3. Add creamed butter to dry ingredients and beat thoroughly.
4. Refrigerate dough for 1 hour.
5. Preheat oven to 300° F (150° C).
6. Shape chilled dough into 1-inch balls.
7. Place balls about 1 1/2 inches apart on ungreased cookie sheets.
8. Flatten slightly with a lightly floured fork.
9. Bake for about 20 minutes or until

edges are lightly browned. *Do not overbake.*

10. Serve with a cup of tea and a dollop of nonmalicious gossip. Enjoy!

ABOUT THE AUTHOR

Nancy Atherton is the bestselling author of twenty-one other Aunt Dimity mysteries. The first book in the series, *Aunt Dimity's Death*, was voted "One of the Century's 100 Favorite Mysteries" by the Independent Mystery Booksellers Association. She lives in Colorado Springs, Colorado.

The employees of Thorndike Press hope you have enjoyed this Large Print book. All our Thorndike, Wheeler, and Kennebec Large Print titles are designed for easy reading, and all our books are made to last. Other Thorndike Press Large Print books are available at your library, through selected bookstores, or directly from us.

For information about titles, please call:
(800) 223-1244

or visit our website at:
gale.com/thorndike

To share your comments, please write:
Publisher
Thorndike Press
10 Water St., Suite 310
Waterville, ME 04901